ANGELS OF THE KNIGHTS

~FALLON~

VALERIE ZAMBITO

Cover Art by Elena Dudina

www.elenadudina.com

OTHER TITLES BY VALERIE ZAMBITO

ISLAND SHIFTERS - AN OATH OF THE BLOOD (BOOK 1)

ISLAND SHIFTERS - AN OATH OF THE MAGE (BOOK 2)

ISLAND SHIFTERS - AN OATH OF THE CHILDREN (BOOK 3)

ANGELS OF THE KNIGHTS - FALLON (BOOK 1)

ANGELS OF THE KNIGHTS - BLANE (BOOK2)

CLASSROOM HEROES

ANGELS OF THE KNIGHTS SERIES REVIEWS

"THE STORY WAS INSANE. ONCE FALLON LEAVES EMPERICA TO HEAD BACK TO EARTH AS A KNIGHT, YOU BETTER STRAP YOURSELF IN FOR THE RIDE".

"I COULDN'T PUT IT DOWN!!!!!!!!!!!!"

"I ATE THIS BOOK UP! I THOROUGHLY ENJOYED THE AUTHOR'S STYLE OF WRITING AND THE NEW PREMISE THIS BOOK HAD."

TABLE OF CONTENTS

PROLOGUE

Fallon - 1978

"Who is she?" the doctor asked as he ran alongside the gurney.

"Fallon Angell. Fifteen years old. Gunshot to the chest. Home invasion."

"Her parents?"

"Dead. Along with a younger brother. She is the sole survivor."

My parents are dead? Gregory is dead?

The doctor grunted. "Be careful, she's not a survivor yet, nurse. Going in to scrub. Meet you inside."

Wait. Yes. Two men wearing masks entered our home. They surprised us as we were watching television, but I can't remember anything else after that.

The gurney pushed through two swinging doors with a loud bang, and Fallon had to squint in the glare of bright overhead lights. An operating room, she realized.

People in masks shouted frantic orders, and she could feel their rushed movement around the room. Despite the harsh light above her, darkness at the edges of her vision slowly crept inward. Her body felt heavy, and it was difficult to move.

"Grab the bottom! One, two, three!"

Hands reached out and roughly yanked at the sheet beneath her, lifting her onto a cold, metal table. Surprisingly, she did not feel any pain, just that unfamiliar heaviness in her chest that made her feel as though she was slowly sinking into quicksand.

Beep. Beep. Beep.

"We're losing her! Where is the damn doctor?"

Are they talking about me? Why can't I remember everything that happened?

"He's still in scrub!"

Beep. Beep.

"Tell him to hurry!"

The quicksand continued to pull at her greedily with insistent, hungry fingers, and the bright white lights of the operating room began to dim further. What little energy she had left slowly leeched away from her body.

"Paddles!"

With abrupt finality, the operating lights disappeared.

"It's not working! Doctor!"

Beep.

Unable to see in the sudden blackness, Fallon started to panic. Gingerly, she lifted her head and noticed a tiny pinpoint of light wink into existence above her. Not the artificial light of the operating room, but different. Pure.

Radiant. There was something incredibly mystical and benevolent about the light, and Fallon's fear melted away, replaced by a strong compulsion to move toward it.

"I'm here!" the doctor yelled. "Did you use the paddles?"

"It's too late. She's gone."

The light beckoned to Fallon, and she smiled as her body lifted off the operating table. There was joy in that light, and she was anxious to see where it would lead. She willingly left the worry, and the heaviness, and the screaming attendants behind and glided toward the light.

A yelp of surprise tore from her throat when she felt herself wrenched forward through the inky blackness as though being pulled by a magnetic force. The air sliced over her body as she picked up speed, but for reasons she could not explain, she did not feel afraid. Glancing to the left and right, she noticed she was in a tunnel of some sort and not alone. Several people floated alongside her, and their faces showed a variety of emotion. Some looked frightened, others peaceful, and a few shouted out with laughter as if they were on a high-speed rollercoaster ride. Most, like her, were simply curious.

As she drew closer to the white light, it dissolved into individual beacons of illumination and finally into white-robed figures, all waiting at the end of the black tunnel.

One waved to her. "Fallon Angell! Over here! Fallon! Come this way!"

Hesitantly, she glided out of the tunnel into what she could only describe as white nothingness. There was no up or down, no sky or horizon of any kind. Nothing but pure whiteness.

Confused people milled around while the figures called out other names enthusiastically. Fallon went to the man who continued to motion to her. With light hair and a slightly lined face, he appeared to be middle aged and greeted her with a beaming smile.

"Hello, Fallon. My name is Josiah and I am an Aegian. I will be your guide to Emperica."

"Emperica?"

"Yes, my dear, that is the proper name although most humans call it heaven. Some refer to it as the Pearly Gates. A few, the Golden Arches." He paused and tilted his head. "No, no, that's not it. Mortals of your day use that name for something else, don't they?"

She nodded. "McDonald's."

"McDonald's? What is that?"

"It's a fast food restaurant," she admitted with embarrassment.

"A fast, what?" Before she could answer, he shrugged and waved a hand in the air dismissively. "Nevertheless, the proper name is indeed Emperica."

"So, I am dead?"

"I am afraid so."

"My parents and brother?"

"Oh, they came through already and are off with their guides. You may run into them again at some point, but right now, I must get you to the gates. Hurry, now, there are quite a few people arriving, and we have been instructed to keep the flow moving." He glided away from her, but stopped when he realized she was not following.

"Is something wrong, Fallon?"

"I...this is a lot to take in. I mean, I really can't believe I'm actually dead. I want to see my family and make sure they are all right."

Josiah gave her a sympathetic smile. "I am sorry, Fallon, please forgive me. Your family is fine. All will be made clear once you arrive in Emperica. I promise."

Feeling like she had no other choice, she nodded.

Josiah led the way to several more tunnels, but instead of black, these were of the same dazzling white. With a kind smile, he reached back for her hand and as soon as she took it, her feet left the ground and they floated together through the entrance of one of the tunnels.

"We only have a few moments, but I will explain a few things to you in the time that we do have. In case you have not figured it out yet, you are an angel."

She nodded again. "I sort of figured that, but did not want to assume."

"Now, in Emperica, there are four castes of angels. The largest group is the Patrit Caste, we call them the Paties, and they are the main society of angels. They see to the administrative affairs of the realm. The second largest caste is the Sentinel Caste, and they are the guardian angels. Next, there is the Aegian Caste, of which yours truly is a member," he said proudly, "and we are the guides. We are responsible for leading all new angels to the gates. Lastly, there is the Knight Caste, and they are the warrior angels."

"Guardian angels?" She thought about all of the times she heard people talk about having a guardian angel looking over their shoulder. "Do these angels ever go back down to earth?"

Josiah nodded. "The guardians spend most of their time on earth, but do come back to Emperica to meet with the Elders from time to time. The Paties and the Aegians never leave Emperica, and the Knights, well, they are a different story altogether. Once they return to earth, they do not come back." He shook his head. "Poor things. Their wings must be clipped because they cannot be in wraith form to kill the Kjin. Instead, they retain their human bodies and become earth angels."

If possible, the light in the tunnel was getting brighter. He pointed ahead. "Look, Fallon, we are almost there!"

"Wait! What is a Kjin?"

Josiah smile turned into a grimace. "Pure evil. Before Mordeaux, or hell, was sealed centuries ago, demons were unleashed into the world and, to this day, they continue to walk the earth causing death and destruction. The Knights seek them out and destroy them."

She had many more questions, but they were slowing.

"I tell you about the four different castes now because you will need to choose one very soon. Are you a guide, a guardian, a warrior or a worker bee, Fallon Angell? Only you can decide."

Their rapid ascent through the tunnel came to an abrupt end and Josiah helped her to step out.

"Welcome home, Fallon."

The tears pooled in Fallon's eyes as she gazed upon the enormous gilded gates of Emperica for the first time. It was more than the beauty of the structure that moved her—it was the depth of emotion that swelled inside her heart. This was a place of unequivocal love and peace and tranquility. Josiah was right. This was home.

"I will leave you now, Fallon. The Paties are waiting on the other side."

Impulsively, she reached out and hugged the Aegian. "Goodbye, Josiah."

He smiled at her. "We will meet again, Fallon. I am sure of it."

Josiah left her then, and Fallon stood among the other new angels as the hallowed gates to Emperica slowly began to open. A ray of light brighter than anything she could ever have imagined flowed through the widening gap, and Fallon lifted her face to allow the radiance to wash over her. She could have stood there forever bathing in that light, but as soon as the gates were fully open, an army of smiling angels walked out to greet them with open arms.

Dressed in a flowing gown of white and a pair of lovely wings fanned out behind her in glorious detail, one angel floated over. Fallon decided then that as long as she existed, she would never be as spectacular and elegant as the angel in front of her.

"Hello, Fallon. My name is Leah, and I am a Patie. I will take you through the process of your choice of caste." She held out an arm and tiny tendrils of mist flowed through the air. "Follow me."

As though moving through a dream, Fallon walked through the realm of Emperica and could only describe it as a veritable paradise in every sense of the word. After the blackness of the first tunnel and the whiteness of the second, the vivid colors were blinding to look at—the hues unlike anything that existed on earth.

She glided beside Leah along a wide path that wound through lush verdant meadows scattered with wildflowers so luminescent that they did not seem to be solid. Birds of every variety sang while they dipped and played in the air overhead, their trilling calls magical to the ear. Animals and children romped together in the sunshine, and blue waterfalls splashed into rivers that sparkled with life.

Wherever she looked, the scenery filled her vision with unimaginable beauty.

Leah's soft voice drew her attention. "It is magnificent, is it not?"

"Yes."

Leah gave her a comforting smile and her blue eyes twinkled. "I remember my first day. Goodness, it was almost one hundred years ago now, but if feels like yesterday."

"May I ask where we are going?" Fallon dared to ask.

"First, you will acquire your wings and then you must decide which caste you wish to join." She turned her ethereal face to Fallon. "Have you decided yet?"

Fallon shook her head. "No...not yet. I am still trying to figure everything out."

"We are here," Leah whispered reverently and stopped in front of wide stone stairs that seemed to appear out of nowhere.

"Here?" Fallon asked. "Where is here?"

Leah pointed up the stairs, and Fallon gasped loudly. Standing at the top was a tall figure immersed in a halo of light. He wore a white robe and had white, shoulder length hair and a short beard. His kindly gaze swept over the new angels, and Fallon knew instantly that she was loved by his man beyond anything in her reference as a human being.

This was the Creator.

His eyes were the most remarkable feature about him. Full of unconditional love, yes, but also wise and all knowing as his focused stare took in the newcomers. And, as much love as she could feel coming from the figure, Fallon also knew that he was capable of incredible wrath. Not for the angels of Emperica or the mortals of earth, but for the evil that stalked them and threatened them with harm.

Leah pressed her hand into Fallon's back and urged her forward with a smile.

Fallon waited in line as one by one the Creator welcomed each angel into his open arms, swallowing them whole in the aura of his light. As each angel emerged from that glorious embrace, Fallon noticed newly formed wings protruding from their backs.

By the time it was her turn, Fallon glided into the Creator's arms eagerly and tears poured down her face from the sheer joy that flowed into her body.

Welcome home, child.

The words were spoken inside her mind instead of aloud.

Hello, Father.

His embrace felt like a cocoon of warmth and tenderness.

Your mortal mother came to me just moments ago.

Is she okay, Father?

Of course. She wanted me to know that you are a very special angel, and she thanked me for granting her the opportunity to be your mother for the short time she had you.

Fallon continued to cry tears of happiness and, no matter how hard she tried, she could not stop.

You will not see her as often as you did on earth, as she will be pursuing her own spiritual path just as you will follow yours.

Fallon nodded. The knowledge did not upset her. The singular love she had for her small family on earth was quickly being replaced by an all-encompassing devotion to the Creator and all of the angels in Emperica.

Choose your path wisely, Fallon. Your mother was correct. You are special.

Thank you, Father.

He released her then and she drifted back down the stairs to make room for the next angel. With a shrug of her shoulders, the back of her shirt ripped open and a majestic pair of wings unfurled behind her. A dizzying sensation of weightlessness coursed through her, and she lifted off the ground with every step she took. She was so giddy with pleasure that she wanted nothing more than to take flight and soar into the clouds.

Leah flitted to her side. "Your choice of caste, Fallon. I know you have not had a lot of time, but you..."

"I do not need any more time, Leah. I know what caste I want to join." There could be no doubt as to what her path would be. "I want to become a Knight."

In the Creator's embrace, she felt his fury for the Kjin that walked the earth and wanted more than anything to aid him in his eternal battle against evil.

But, there was another reason to fight. One that was equally as compelling.

She finally remembered what happened to her the night she died.

34 Years Later

CHAPTER 1

The Girl

The girl had no idea that she was in mortal danger. Like a typical teenager of this age, she talked animatedly into the phone she carried, oblivious to her surroundings. She probably felt safe walking the main street of this small, active college town. The unusually warm fall night brought out many of the students, and she passed them by as they stood in large groups in front of the store fronts laughing and horsing around. One boy called out to the girl, and she waved back distractedly as she turned onto a less populated side street.

Fallon shadowed the girl's movements, trying to anticipate from which angle the attack would come.

The Kjin was very near.

She could sense his desire.

He wanted the girl.

The Kur on her arm heated which meant the hunger of the Kjin was growing.

Fallon quickly took off her hoodie and tied it around her waist, pulling the Aventi from the back pocket of her jeans. The girl, still lost in conversation, turned down a dead end road. Had she looked up, she would have noticed that the street light was out. The Kjin obviously had been stalking this girl for some time and knew her habits.

Out of the corner of Fallon's eye, she noticed a young man approach the girl from the opposite side of the street. His boyish good looks did not fool her and it was not just because her Kur erupted into a flaming sear on her arm. Even from this distance, she could see the evil in his eyes.

The man crossed the street, and Fallon started to sprint. Focused on his prey, the Kjin did not see her. He walked up to the girl just as she ended her conversation and was putting the cell phone into her book bag. Smiling at her disarmingly, he caught her off guard when his fist lashed out and struck her in the face. Before she fell, he grabbed her around the neck and clamped his hand over her mouth. The girl dropped her book bag and struggled against his tight grip, but he was too strong and was able to drag her behind the garage of a house with darkened windows with little effort.

"Shut up!" he whispered harshly at the girl, and she did so immediately. Fallon could tell that she was terrified.

"What do you want?" she asked with a voice crackling in fear.

He pressed her up against the side of the garage and ran his tongue slowly up the side of her cheek. "I want you."

"Please, don't," she whimpered.

The Kjin pulled back to look at her with a sneer and reached down for the button of her jeans. "Just do as I say and afterwards I'll let you go. Do you understand?"

The girl choked back a sob, but nodded.

Fallon stepped out of the shadows. "Let her go."

The Kjin whipped his head toward her, but did not release his prize. He had no way of knowing that Fallon was a Knight. "Get out of here or you'll be next," he growled at her.

"Not likely," she murmured and slammed the Aventi against the Kur on her arm. The night lit up with the brilliance of the sword as it flared in the dim recess at the side of the garage. The girl's eyes widened as much as the Kjin's. Hers held fright and his recognition.

The Kjin rammed the girl's head into the side of the garage and she crumbled to the ground. He turned to face Fallon. "You don't know who you're dealing with," he commented through thin cruel lips.

"Nor do I care," she responded and lunged with supernatural speed. He tried to dodge the thrust, but she was too quick and the sword pierced his side. He hissed in pain but managed to spin in a circle and bring his leg around toward her head. With her left hand, she caught his ankle in a vise-like grip inches from her face. With her right, she sliced his throat.

He made a clumsy attempt to hit her with his fist, but he was already dying from the cut she made, so she let go of his ankle and pushed him to the ground.

His death did not take long and within seconds, a black, snarling wraith exploded out of the corpse, searching for a nearby body to steal. It roared menacingly when its eyes found Fallon, but she did not hesitate. She plunged the Aventi into the center of the dark mass and it disintegrated into a pile of ash.

The threat eliminated, she walked over to the body of the young man the demon inhabited and looked down at him with sadness. His head lolled to the side and his eyes were glazed over in death but already she could see the change in him. His face showed such innocence now. She wondered when the Kjin took his body. Was he a child at the time? Was it more recent? Had his family detected the changes in his personality and wondered at the cause?

She knelt by his side and whispered, "Your Aegian guide awaits you, my child. There, you will find your peace."

Whoever found his earthly body would assume he died of natural causes. That would be better for the parents to accept than the fact that a demon had been dwelling there. All that Fallon cared about was that there was one less Kjin in the world. They could not reproduce so every one slain was a step closer to having an earth free of evil.

The girl moaned.

Fallon quickly went to her, picked her up and brought her back to the sidewalk. As soon as the girl opened her eyes, Fallon waved the Aventi before her eyes. The pupils dilated and went out of focus for a moment and then regained their vision.

"Are you all right?" Fallon asked.

"Yes, I think so," she said, getting to her feet. "What happened?"

Fallon refused to lie. "It looks like you took a blow to your head."

"I...I must have tripped and blacked out."

She did not correct her. "Can I help you home?"

The girl shakily picked up her book bag and slung it over her arm. "No, I...I think I am all right. I live just down the street. Thank you for your help."

"No problem. But, hey, be careful next time, okay?"

The girl gave her a grateful smile and walked away.

Fallon turned and went back the way she had come. She was late now for her meeting with Father Tomas at St. Mary's Cathedral Church, but she had not expected to find a Kjin here so quickly.

Hurrying along, Fallon decided she liked this little upstate New York college town of Alden. It was peaceful and quaint with the requisite non-working fountain smack in the center of Main Street. Old and stately homes dotted the surrounding streets, many of which had been converted into apartments for the students that flooded into the area every fall.

Fallon untied the sweatshirt from around her waist and shrugged into it, pulling the hood over her head. Back on Main Street, she passed through the crowd of students without making eye contact, but their easy companionship did make her long for Julian and Nikki, the only friends she had here on earth. Any friends Fallon had prior to her death were most likely busy making plans for retirement or caring for grandchildren.

Still, she did not feel envious. She was following her calling and knew that Darius was pleased with her efforts to eradicate the Kjin and save human lives. With a smile, she thought back to her first day of Knight training.

Leah, the Patie, left her after she received her wings, so Fallon walked into the vast arched doors of the Hall of Knights on her own. Beneath a domed ceiling at least one hundred feet high, male and female angels engaged in a variety of combat drills. Some were learning defensive moves and others were being lectured in small groups. Most, however, were sparring with a sword of light. The speed and agility with which the angels moved was otherworldly, and Fallon wondered if she, too, would have these same abilities when her training was complete.

The door opened behind her and three angels, two boys and a girl, similar to her age walked into the hall. They immediately approached her. "Are you going to train to be a Knight?" one asked, a tall, blonde-haired boy.

She nodded.

"My name is Julian," he told her. "And, these two are Blane and Nikki." Blane was also tall but with dark hair,

and Nikki had her long auburn hair pulled back into a high ponytail.

"Hi, I'm Fallon."

She was about to ask them questions when a male angel dressed in white pants and a sleeveless white shirt belted around the middle with a tie glided toward them. At least seven feet in height, he was much larger and glowed brighter than anyone else in the room.

Julian nudged her and whispered. "He is an Elder."

"What's an Elder?" she asked.

"There are four Elders in total, one for each caste. I guess you could say he is our new boss."

"Welcome angels," the Elder greeted in a rumbling, deep voice. "My name is Darius and I am the Elder for the Knight Caste." He reached into a bag with a drawstring that hung from his belt. He handed each one of them a gold cuff. "You are to wear this on your arm at all times during training. It is called a Kur and it goes without saying that it is a device of great power." Reaching back into the bag, he handed them another object. To Fallon, it looked like nothing more than a simple black tube. "This is your Aventi. Your sword. To ignite its power, you simply touch the Aventi against the Kur on your arm. I will demonstrate." Darius stepped back and tapped the black tube he held to the Kur around his bicep. Immediately, a sword of light burst into existence with a slight humming sound. He slammed the hilt of the Aventi against the Kur once again and the motion extinguished the white beam.

"Amazing," breathed Nikki.

"You will learn more as you train, but I will give you a little background now before we begin. Back in the early days of the world's creation, a sinister presence developed from the seed of man. His name was Tyras, and he was very successful at whispering dark insinuations into the ears of the flawed men and women of earth. Soon, he developed a large following of evildoers. The Creator discovered what Tyras was up to and banished him and his followers into the underworld of Mordeaux. Many years later, Tyras discovered a way to break out of his prison and let loose thousands of his demonic brethren into the world. The Creator was able to capture Tyras and send him back to Mordeaux where he sealed him once again into his underworld prison, but the others, we call the Kjin, were not so easy to find. They appear as normal people, but are not. They are the murderers, the rapists, and the terrorists that live to torment humans. The evil wraiths live in the host bodies of those they kill, and when that body dies, they simply move on to another. If not for these creatures, there would be very little sin on earth."

He paused to make sure his young audience was listening.

"The only weapon that can kill the Kjin is the Aventi of a Knight of Emperica."

"How many Knights are there?" Blane asked.

"Very few are chosen," Darius admitted. "Very few develop the skills necessary to defeat the Kjin. It remains to be seen whether the four of you will become Knights."

Fallon's small group murmured anxiously.

"My guide mentioned that if I become a Knight, my wings will be clipped and I will be earthbound," Nikki commented with a shudder.

Darius nodded. *"It is not a pleasant experience, I am afraid, as the sacrifice of an angel's wings can never be made lightly. But, there are two reasons why it is important. The first is of simple necessity. You must have a corporeal form to wield the Aventi. The second is that the pain of wing removal serves as a reminder of the commitment you wish to undertake. Mortals are completely defenseless against the Kjin and their only protection are the Knights of this caste. If you succeed in your goal of Knighthood, you will not return to Emperica again until you die a natural death, which for earth angels will not happen for a very long time, or you are killed. If a Kjin does manage to kill you, you will return to Emperica and become a member of the Patrit Caste."*

"A Patie! But, I don't want to be a Patie!" exclaimed Julian.

Darius patted him on the shoulder. *"Then I suggest that you do not die again, young angel."*

Fallon felt a sense of pride fill her at the thought of returning to earth and saving humans from the Kjin. She was even thinking of seeing her old friends again. *"How long does the training take, Elder?"*

"Thirty years."

CHAPTER 2

The Emissier & The Cop

"Forgive me Father, for I have sinned. It has been four days since my last confession."

Fallon could not see the Emissier's face beyond the screened window, but did hear him chuckle softly. "You are forgiven, child, although I doubt very much you have anything to be forgiven for."

She smiled in the dark of the small confessional. "No."

"Thank you for coming, Fallon. Darius tells me that you have proven yourself to be one of the best Knights we have."

"I do what I can, Father."

"That is good to hear, because we have a particularly dangerous Kjin in this area. Two children have gone missing within the past month, but before that, the Kjin was killing college-aged girls. A total of six over the past fifteen years that I can with almost certainty attribute to him."

"Are you sure it's the same Kjin, Father? It would be unusual for a serial killer of women to suddenly resort to crimes against children."

The dark silhouette nodded. "It is the same one. I know this because he is now leaving a calling card."

"He's taunting the police?" Fallon asked in surprise.

"No. Me."

The news shocked her. "You? What type of calling card does he leave?"

"Flowers. A lily dipped in fresh blood was placed on the rectory steps after each child disappeared."

Fallon's blood raged at the thought of this Kjin killing innocent women and children. "Luck may be with us, Father. I killed a Kjin just before I came here and it could have been the one you are looking for."

The priest stiffened.

"It was a young man," she continued, "and he attempted to abduct a girl right off the street."

Father Tomas shook his head. "No. This Kjin is quite a few years older. But, I will admit that it is highly unusual to have another in the immediate area. The Kjin have never come together as an organized faction which means these animals are very territorial about their dens of destruction."

A sudden detail came to Fallon's mind. "How do you know how old he is?"

The Emissier paused. "Because I know who he is. He is the President and a professor at Alden University with a wife and four children. I have personally known him for over twenty years and never once suspected him of being Kjin until three weeks ago when he carelessly walked too close to the font and a splash of holy water sizzled on his hand from the contact. He tried to quickly cover his mistake, but not before I saw it happen."

"What is his name?"

"Marc Ellis, and for this particular assignment, you will pose as a college student to get closer to him. He is very intelligent, Fallon, so I must warn you how difficult this will be." The shadow leaned in close to the screen. "He has already killed another Knight, Fallon. A man named Gabe Mackey."

Fallon sucked in her breath. "A Ha'Basin?" The Ha'Basin was a ritual of dark magic that required ten Kjin working in concert to invoke the power necessary to cast a Knight back to Emperica. It was an almost impossible feat to get a Knight into a weakened position to allow that to happen and even more rare for that many Kjin to be working together.

"No, not a Ha'Basin. Gabe was drugged and killed."

Again, her anger flared. "I will handle this, Father."

The priest's voice turned urgent. "Please be careful, Fallon, I do not wish to lose another Knight."

She nodded but did not respond, already planning the Kjin's demise in her mind.

"Go to AU, get close to the man, and choose your opportunity carefully. Your registration is complete and you simply need to go to the Registrar's Office tomorrow morning to pick up your schedule."

"Do you have a place for me to stay?"

A white paper appeared under the screen. "Here is the address. Just two blocks from here, it is an old, yellow Victorian. It is quite large for one person, but all I could arrange with the short notice I had. It is very hard to find housing at this time of year." An envelope slid toward her. "Here is the key and money. I have already stocked a few groceries in the house, but was not sure of your preferences."

"I am sure they will be fine. Thank you, Father," she said, standing. "I will be back in touch in a few days."

"Wait! I need you to do one other thing for me if you would."

She sat back down. "Of course."

"It is a personal favor. There is a young former police officer at the jailhouse named Kade Royce. He is being released today after spending the past year in jail. His parents are out of the country, and I promised to deliver this key to Kade for his new apartment which happens to be right next door to yours." Father Tomas passed another envelope to her. "He is also attending AU this fall."

She reached for the envelope. "What did he do to end up in jail?"

"Let's just say he was too good at his job. He had an uncanny ability to ferret out the criminals in this county, and, unfortunately, the top Kjin took notice and set him up on fake drug charges."

"This Marc Ellis?"

"The very same. Gabe Mackey was posing as a police officer alongside Kade, and the two made quite a pair before the set up. Fortunately, an undercover police officer got to Kade and arrested him before he could be killed. Gabe was not so lucky."

"Things are a lot more complicated than I thought."

"That they are, Fallon. Thank you for doing this and, again, please be careful."

She nodded and then stood, pulled back the black curtain of the confessional stall and stepped out. The church was silent at this hour, but a sudden movement caught her eye. An altar boy dressed in a white cassock was taking a seat in the last pew to pray. Fallon left him to his private moment and pushed out of the wide double doors of the church.

She looked at the small paper in her hand.

Yellow Victorian at 47 Oak Street

She already knew where Oak Street was from her earlier walk through the small town, but headed in the opposite direction toward the county jailhouse.

Navigating once again through the teenaged mob, Fallon could feel their excitement in the air. For most of these kids, this was their first time being out on their own. Not yet bogged down with the deluge of work that would keep many of them confined to their dorms or apartments for long hours after the term started, tonight was a night for celebration.

Soon, she would be among them but was not looking forward to it. She had little in common with young adults her age and not entirely comfortable in social situations the way she used to be. After more than thirty years away, she was still trying to wrap her mind around that fact that you could talk on a phone without wires and that parachute pants and platform shoes had gone out of style. Whenever she made an attempt at conversation, it was inevitable that she would make a comment that would cause people to look at her funny. The problem was, she was never quite sure which one was the offending comment so that she could correct it for the next time.

Julian tried to help as he was having no such trouble. Apparently, it was much easier for him to assimilate back into this society. He was smooth and polished, and acted as if he had been born in the 1990's instead of the 1960's.

With a fond smile, she shook away thoughts of her friend and entered the jailhouse, a nineteenth century red brick building with huge white pillars out front.

The young deputy behind the desk immediately straightened. "Can I help you?"

"I'm here for Kade Royce."

His face registered shock, but he tried to hide it. He directed her to a bench along the wall. "Have a seat. He will be out in a few minutes."

She turned from the desk and sat down, but noticed the guard glancing her way every few seconds, clearly curious as to who she was. Alden was a very small town and the deputy not only must have worked with this Kade guy, but probably knew him personally.

Well, he would have to keep guessing.

The door behind the deputy buzzed open and a young man in faded jeans and white tee shirt strode out. He was about six foot, muscular throughout the shoulders and chest, but with narrow hips and legs. His dark hair was too long, and he needed a shave, but it did not hide the obvious—he was drop dead gorgeous. He walked with a primal and authoritative grace that belied his young age, which if she had to guess was about twenty-three or four.

He threw some papers down on the desk. "Everything is there, Dave. I'm out," and he walked toward the door without waiting for a response.

"Um...Kade."

Kade turned back impatiently. "What is it?"

Dave the deputy nodded his head toward Fallon. "She's here for you."

Kade turned and looked at her and then shrugged. "For whatever reason you're here, let's talk about it outside. I need fresh air."

Fallon nodded in understanding and walked over to where he stood, holding the door open for her. She felt her face flush when she passed by him. His presence was just so raw and masculine.

When they were out on the street, he looked up at the sky and breathed a sigh of relief and she could see the tension visibly go out of his body. Then, he turned to her. "So, who are you?"

His eyes were a remarkable, pale blue. "I...I'm Fallon Angell. Father Tomas sent me to deliver this." She handed him the envelope. "Keys and the address to your new apartment."

Their fingers brushed when he took the envelope from her, and the electricity generated by their touch surprised them both.

Kade recovered first. "He shouldn't have worried about it. I already know where I'm going. My friends visited me last week. I'll be rooming with them."

"I guess your parents wanted him to make sure you got settled in after being...," she hesitated.

"Incarcerated. You can say it. Never be afraid of the truth, Fallon," he admonished with a playful grin.

Were those dimples?

"Are you a college student?" he asked.

"Yes."

"Well, nice to meet you, Fallon. Thanks for bringing this," he said, holding up the envelope.

"My house is actually right next to yours, so I'll just walk with you if you don't mind." Did that really just come out of her mouth?

"A pretty girl walking me home after a year in jail? Yeah, I think I can deal with that."

She blushed again. Why did she keep doing that?

In silence, they made their way through Main Street and then turned onto Second Street.

"Where are you from?" he finally asked.

"Buffalo."

"How old are you?"

"Nineteen."

"You don't talk much, do you?"

Now, she grinned. "Not really."

He laughed and then they turned onto Oak Street. "What number are you?"

"Forty-seven."

Pointing, he said, "It's the yellow one up on the left. Mine is the white one next door."

"Thanks." She moved to walk past him again, and he grabbed her arm.

"Hey, my buddies are having a little get together tonight if you're interested. Grab your roommates and come over."

"I don't have any roommates."

"No? Well, come on over anyway."

"I...I can't, but thanks."

"So, you're going to be stuck up and not hang out with your new neighbors?" he teased. "Is that it?"

"Are you going to let me go?" she asked, glancing pointedly at his hand on her arm.

"Not unless you agree to come."

"Okay, maybe. Can I leave now?"

He let go of her and stepped aside. "By the way, remember my name, Fallon Angell, because I'm pretty sure I'm going to be the one that brings you back down to earth."

Her head whipped around, but he was already moving away, chuckling softly.

CHAPTER 3

A Friendly Visit

Fallon pulled out the key provided by Father Tomas and unlocked the door to the next on her long list of temporary housing. The old Victorian opened into a foyer with a narrow staircase, scuffed hard wood floors, and decorative crown molding on the walls. And—just like all of the other places she had lived in the past four years—it was deafeningly quiet.

She took time to explore the downstairs that consisted of a large old kitchen, living room and formal dining room, and then went up the steep stairs to the second floor. There were four bedrooms, and Fallon chose the smallest for herself. She was not sure how long she would be living here, but the smaller room had a fireplace that would make the room cozy if the weather turned chilly before she moved on.

She dropped her backpack and fell back onto the old-fashioned canopy bed, her body sinking into its pillowy depths. As always when she entered a new, empty house, her thoughts turned to her family and the night they were all murdered.

It was thirty-four years ago now and it had been a balmy fall evening, just like today, and the front door was left wide open. It was the seventies and no one locked their doors. Everyone was welcome to enter. It was not as if there had been less crime, she had come to realize, it was just that the people were more innocent to the evils of the world back then.

She remembered it like it was yesterday.

Right before the invasion, her family was gathered in their living room watching a television show called Laverne and Shirley. Fallon was singing the catchy theme song along with her younger brother, Gregory—something about hasenpfeffer and making dreams come true. Her mother was crocheting an afghan and Fallon could still see her agonized frown when one stitch did not come out the way she wanted. Her father was reading the paper, but his eyes were drooping and he was about to fall asleep.

Such an innocent scene and all taken away by two Kjin.

They entered with guns drawn, demanding money from her father. When he did not respond fast enough, one struck him across the temple with the butt of his gun. Her mother screamed out and received a blow to the face for it. Furious, Gregory picked up a lamp and hit one of the assailants. The gun was turned on him first and discharged. Blood sprayed across the room from the hole that was ripped into her brother's chest, and he went flying back.

The Kjin who murdered him callously commented that they had to get out of there now and leave no witnesses behind. They shot her father next and then her mother.

Fallon remembered sitting frozen in fear as the gun turned her way. She did not scream. She did not try to run away. She never moved a muscle as the trigger was pulled. The next thing she remembered was waking up on a gurney at Brown Community Hospital.

She scrubbed away a tear. She missed her family so very much. During her years in Emperica, she rarely saw them but never felt the need with all of the love and light that enveloped her in a constant warm, soothing layer. But now, human again, all of her mortal insecurities, doubts, and a painful psychological desire for companionship surged through her. Alone most of the time, she longed for the comfort of home.

The tears began to streak down her face now, and she let them. After four years of the ritual of remembrance and pain, she knew the tide of emotion had to run its natural course.

Suddenly, her body twitched out of its reverie as the door downstairs banged open. She jumped from her bed noiselessly, removed the Aventi from her pocket, and shrugged free of her hoodie so that her Kur was clear.

Creeping silently to the door of her bedroom, she paused and listened. No sound. Cautiously, she peered out into the hall. Again, she did not hear anything. Maybe the wind caused the door to open? She shook her head. No, she could clearly sense the presence of someone in the house.

Besides the Ha'Basin, she did not have much to fear here on earth. Her angelic powers gave her enhanced strength, speed and healing ability. She would recover from almost any internal trauma including broken bones and even a gunshot, but since she would be vulnerable while she healed, it was best not to find herself in that situation.

Slowly, she made her way down the old stairs, and she gritted her teeth as the wood creaked under every light step she took. Hugging the wall, she scanned the hall and living room, but there was no one in sight.

The front door was still open and she looked outside once before walking toward the kitchen.

Just as she crossed the threshold, two strong hands gripped her by the shoulders. Drawing the Aventi, she touched it to the Kur and the weapon blazed to life.

"Whoa! Put that thing away, it's just me!"

Fallon spun away from the offender with a glare.

It was Julian.

She breathed a sigh of relief and extinguished the Aventi. "What are you doing here?"

"Nice to see you, too."

"If you try knocking next time, I'm pretty sure you'll get a much warmer reception."

"Sorry." He held his arms out to her. "Come here."

She finally smiled and walked into his embrace. At six foot four, he towered over her five foot four inch height. His hair was out of style at shoulder length, but he wore it well. Especially, since the new Thor movie came out and he looked very much like the hot lead actor.

"It's good to see you," she admitted, lifting her head to look up at him. "It's been way too long."

His hand came out and he rubbed a thumb across her cheek. "What's this?"

She shook her head. "Nothing."

"Fallon, what is it? I'm your friend. If something is bothering you, I want you to tell me."

"Honestly, it's nothing. I just get a little sad when coming to a new house, that's all."

"You miss your family?"

"Yes."

"Me, too. But, once I remember how happy they are, I forget about it."

Typical Julian. The life of the party. Mr. Sociable. He never let anything keep him down for long.

She pulled out of his embrace. "So, what have you been up to?"

"I feel like I've been spinning my wheels," he snapped irritably. "Do you ever wonder if we'll eventually get a leg up with the Kjin? It's almost as if they are multiplying even though that's not possible."

"It does feel like that some days, but we just have to keep the faith that what we do matters." She walked over to the refrigerator. "Soda? I should have something in here."

"Yeah, I'll take a Dew if you have it."

She found the soda, handed him the can and they sat at her kitchen table.

"When did you get here?" he asked.

"Just a few minutes ago. How did you find me? Father Tomas?"

He nodded. "I went to see him first."

"So, what brings you out this way besides my charming personality?" Since Julian lived and worked mostly in the New York City area, she did not get to see him as much as she would have liked.

He rubbed the back of his neck. "Tracking a Kjin this way, but I lost him. Since I was already out this far, I decided to come see you."

She smiled. "I'm glad you did. Are you spending the night?"

"Yeah, if that's okay. Then, I'll head back home in the morning." He got up to rummage through the kitchen cabinets. "So, what's for dinner?"

She laughed. "I don't even know what I have yet."

They ended up making a quick dinner of frozen pizza and potato chips and headed into the living room to watch television. After two reality shows, Julian began to prowl. "What is there to do around here?"

"How would I know? You know I don't really hang out with people."

"You act like you're fifty years old!"

"I am fifty years old! Come on, Julian, what can I possibly have in common with teenagers?"

"You *are* a teenager, Fallon. Nineteen to be exact. The years training in Emperica don't count here."

"I know," she relented. "I do feel like a teenager still, but really Julian, a Knight that gives in to teenage angst? I don't think that would work out very well."

"Well, we have to do *something*."

For some reason, her heart started racing. "I did get invited to a party next door tonight."

"By who?"

"A guy."

Julian straightened and ran his hands through his hair. "Now, we're talking. How do I look? There's got to be some hot college chicks at this party, right?"

"I don't think they call girls *chicks* any more. Besides, I didn't say I was going, I said I was invited."

"Oh, we're going."

"Julian..."

"Your boyfriend won't mind if I tag along, will he?"

"He's not my boyfriend!" she exploded. "But, from what I know of college parties, they're pretty much a free-for-all."

His gaze roamed her body. "You're not wearing that, are you?"

She looked down at her sweats and sneakers. "What's wrong with this?"

He waved a hand at her. "It's lame. Where are your clothes?" He started up the stairs to her bedroom.

She ran after him. "I don't have much! I only brought a few things with me from my apartment."

He looked in all of the rooms until he came to the one with her bag. Rifling through it, he found a pair of skinny jeans. "Wear these and a pair of flip flops."

She ripped the jeans from his hand. "What am I dressing up for?"

"Duh, your boyfriend."

"Say it again and the Aventi comes out," she growled.

Julian did keep his mouth closed, but continued to stand there staring at her.

"Oh, all right! But, this will probably be the last time I'll ever see the guy. Without a doubt, I'll say something stupid and he will give me that look I have seen a thousand times, and I will be on my solitary way. End of story." She paused. "Although, he did say something weird."

"What?"

"He said he was going to be the one to bring me back down to earth."

"Ooh, maybe he's an Intuit and knows you're an angel." Intuit was the term they used for clairvoyant people who could sense the presence of paranormal beings.

"I doubt a college-aged guy has the awareness necessary to be an Intuit."

He shrugged. "Hurry up and get dressed. I'm just dying to meet this new boyfriend of yours."

She did not hesitate and the room lit up with the glow of her sword.

CHAPTER 4

First Kiss

Clad in her skinny jeans and flip flops, Fallon walked with Julian toward the white house next door to hers. Music drifted through the open windows and she could see the silhouettes of people through the curtains.

Her stomach clenched. Why did she let Julian talk her into this? There were only two possible outcomes to this evening. Either she would say something idiotic and have to avoid Kade and his roommates for the rest of her time here in Alden, or no one would talk to her and she would spend the evening watching Julian flirt with girls from some isolated corner of the house.

Fortunately, she did not have too much time to think about it as Julian raced up the steps, opened the door without knocking and stepped inside. Even from behind his considerable bulk, she could see that as soon as they walked in, every female eye in the room turned his way.

She had to admit. With his large presence, smoky eyes and ready smile, Julian was an attractive guy. Sidling in after him, her eyes quickly roved over the people at the party, searching for Kade. Was Julian right? Could Kade really be an Intuit? Usually she could tell immediately if a human was an Intuit simply by the odd way they looked at her. She did not sense that with Kade, but then again she had only talked to the guy for a few minutes.

Julian reached back, grabbed her hand, and dragged her through the house to the patio outside. This was where most of the kids were hanging out.

Including Kade.

He was standing and laughing with two friends, but turned and looked at them as soon as they walked outside. The laughter fell from his face when he saw her hand intertwined with Julian's.

His gaze lifted to her face and when his blue eyes met her green eyes, she felt her face redden and dropped Julian's hand.

Really, Angell? Why do you care what Kade-the-gorgeous-ex-cop-Royce thinks of you?

She knew why.

She wanted him to like her.

She longed for another human being to find her attractive. To find her worthy of a moment of shared laughter. Maybe even a tender touch. She spoke to Julian and Nikki a few times a year, but other than that, she did not have any ties in this world.

Suddenly, she felt dizzy and the sky seemed to be closing down, trying to suffocate her. Her heart pounded in her chest. "Be right back, going to the bathroom," she mumbled to Julian and then fled from the patio.

She had to get out of there before she did or said something completely brainless.

Several others had joined the party and she pushed through them toward the door. "Excuse me."

"Hey!"

"Sorry."

The door was right there, and it was open. With little else in her mind except escape, she ran ran for it and ducked outside, greedily gulping in the fresh night air to calm her anxiety.

A strong hand seized her arm.

It was him.

She did not have to turn around to know.

But, she did turn and watched him push the hair over his forehead back in place. His expression was dark.

"So, are you going to just leave your boyfriend here?"

She shook her head. "He's not my boyfriend."

Kade's eyebrows rose in question. "No? Who is he?"

"A friend. I have known him for a very long time," she muttered softly, hoping he did not ask how long because he would never believe the answer. "Nice party, but I have to go." She turned to walk down the steps, but his hand did not let go of her arm.

He leaned down over the back of her to whisper in her ear, and she inhaled the scent of him. It was a clean smell. Like some sort of spicy, masculine soap. "Let me walk you home."

"I...I just live next door," she said hoarsely. "I think I can manage from here."

"It's too crowded in there. I really can't stand enclosed places any more. Come on." And, for the second time that evening, a boy grabbed her hand.

As a Knight, she was used to being in control, but Kade pulled her down the stairs and onto the sidewalk with a commanding stride, and she had no choice but to follow.

Silently, they made the short walk to her yellow Victorian and up the stairs of the porch. Only then did he turn to face her.

On the step above her, he towered over her. Realizing his mistake, the air left her body when he walked back down one stair, picked her up by the waist, and swung her up to the stair above him. Now, she had no choice but to look him in the eye.

"I like you, Fallon."

She grinned nervously. "I think any girl might look good to you right now." The minute the words left her mouth, she cringed.

But, he simply laughed. "No, that's not it. I promise. I don't know how to explain it, but I just feel like there is something special about you, and I would like to get to know you better."

She shook her head. "There's nothing special about me."

"You know that's not true."

An Intuit? She still could not decide. "I guess we can be friends," she told him, acutely aware that his hands were still holding her by the waist.

"Can friends do this?" Lifting one hand, he caressed her cheek and pulled her face closer.

Her breath caught in her throat at the intimate contact. The feeling of his hands on her tapped into an emotional well she thought dried up long ago. Hunger for affection rushed through her and she felt her legs weaken. It had been so long! Could she really do this? Kiss him? Or, would she screw it up like almost everything else connected to humans?

As his head bent to hers, it suddenly no longer mattered. Softly, his lips met hers. Tenderly at first, but then more insistently as his tongue probed her mouth. He moved the hand around her waist to the small of her back and pulled her in closer against his body. Her own hands came up instinctively to stop him, but of their own free will, snaked around his neck.

He let out a moan of pleasure at the same time that the Kur on her arm flared to life with a searing burn. Her head snapped to the side and she pushed him away from her.

Three guys were passing by on the sidewalk in front of her house. She wondered for a brief second if it could be Professor Marc Ellis, but it was not. All three of the men were young.

"Oh, so this is where Kade went. Getting himself a little piece of our new neighbor," one of the guys commented.

Kade turned around and the anger etched into his features was unmistakable. "Have a little respect, Ethan."

Ethan put his hands up. "Hey, I don't blame you, dude. She's gorgeous."

"Just shut up and keep walking, Ethan, or I will be only too happy to help you on your way." Kade moved down one of the steps of her porch to back up his words.

The other two guys on the street grabbed Ethan's arms. "Just ignore him, Kade. We're leaving."

Ethan let himself be propelled down the sidewalk, but Fallon noticed that his eyes did not leave hers for half a block.

"Who is that?" she asked Kade.

"Ethan Kiley, my roommate and supposed best friend."

"What do you mean supposed?"

Kade shook his head. "The guy has been acting really weird all day and even the last time he came to visit me in jail. Not like himself at all. I honestly don't know what's wrong with him. Maybe he's having problems at home."

He is a Kjin, that's his problem, thought Fallon. "Listen, Kade, I really have to get inside."

His eyes held disappointment. "Yeah, me too, I guess. Classes start tomorrow." He paused. "I would like to see you again if you're okay with that."

"I...yes, I would like that."

"Okay, see you tomorrow."

She nodded and went into the house. After closing the door, she ran up the stairs, quickly changed out of her skinny jeans and into black pants and a black hoodie. She slipped the Aventi into her back pocket.

She wished more than anything that she could lie in bed and think of Kade's kiss, think about how good it felt, but she did not have any time to spare.

She had to go and kill his best friend.

CHAPTER 5

Painful Memories

Fallon tossed and turned as she listened to the creaks and rattles of the old Victorian most of the night. It was not just the unfamiliar noises that kept her up. In the darkness, she could deny reality and choose instead to remember how good it felt to have Kade kiss her and put his hands on her. She could forget about their differences and dream about a future together.

But, now, in the harsh brightness of the morning, she could no longer escape the truth.

She could never see Kade again.

Although returned to her human body, it was foolish really to think she could develop a meaningful relationship with anyone. Last night, she had only lost herself in Kade for a few moments and a Kjin managed to get within striking distance. Her focus should be on her duties to all of humankind, she reminded herself, where a single moment of inattention could mean the lives of those she had been entrusted to protect. Darius and the Knights of Emperica put a tremendous amount of time training and honing her skills, and she could not—would not—allow all of their hard work be wasted.

As if to drive the point home, two long scars on her shoulder blades began to throb. The wounds where her wings had been removed pained her most mornings. It was at its worst when she first awoke, but lessened to a dull ache as the day wore on.

It was the agony of that amputation that she remembered now.

"Turn toward the wall and put your hands in the manacles," Darius instructed.

"Is that really necessary?" she asked, suddenly frightened as she stepped into the small room.

"Yes. I will not lie to you, Fallon, the pain will be great. In order to make clean incisions, you must be restrained."

With a deep breath, she stepped over to the wall and lifted her hands to the chains that hung from the wall. Another angel locked the irons over her wrist and then secured her ankles in place into metal rings on the floor.

Nervously, she bit into her lip as she awaited her fate. Darius did not waste any time stepping up behind her. He made three expert cuts in her shirt and it fell away from her body leaving her back bare.

"While this sacrifice is necessary for your chosen path," Darius informed her, "it is not required by the Creator. It is a choice you must make for yourself and should not be made lightly. Are you certain, Fallon Angell, you wish to give up your wings and become a Knight?"

Fallon had already heard the screams from the other angels. Julian had gone through before her and when he came out, his usual smiling face was ashen and tormented. But, her mind was firm.

"Yes."

"Very well." A blazing hot thrust stabbed through her wing, and her back arched as she screamed. It felt like Darius was cutting off her arm. White feathers drifted around the floor next to her as the Elder pulled and cut through her new appendage. By the time he moved to the second wing, she was hanging listlessly from the manacles, no longer able to stand upright. Mercifully, halfway through the removal of this wing, she blacked out.

Fallon shuddered. She only had her wings for a short time, but still missed their beauty and the blissful energy that emanated from them. She shrugged her shoulder blades again with a groan and got out of bed to shower.

Hopefully, she could leave the house without seeing Kade. Right about now, he and his roommates would be wondering where their friend, Ethan, was and why he did not come home last night. She left the body out in the open so he could be discovered quickly. There was no point in prolonging the grief for Ethan's parents and friends.

She wondered why the Kjin picked Ethan. According to Kade, his friend had only started acting differently the past few days so it was a new possession. Was the Kjin simply trading an older body for a younger, healthier one? For some reason, she did not think it was that simple. This was the third Kjin operating in this area, and she had an eerie feeling that she was missing something crucial.

Her cell phone rang, so she stepped out of the shower and grabbed a towel before running back into her room. "Hello."

Surprisingly, it was Julian. She thought he was still asleep in the next room. "It's me. I left early this morning, but didn't want to wake you."

She toweled her hair dry with the phone balanced in the crook of her neck. "No problem. Did you have fun at the party?" He was still not home after she returned from dealing with the Ethan Kjin.

"A gentleman never kisses and tells, Fallon."

"Exactly. That's why I'm asking *you*."

"That hurts."

She laughed. "Keep your secrets then, but don't be such a stranger, okay? Let's get together again sometime before this year ends."

"I'll try. Be careful, Fallon."

"You too," she replied and snapped the phone shut. It took several minutes to get all of the snarls out of her long blonde hair, but as soon as she was done, she dressed and stuffed a pen and notebook into her backpack. It would have to do since that was all she brought from her apartment in Buffalo. How could she have known when she left that she would be attending college?

She hefted the pack and flew down the old Victorian stairs. She took only a moment to grab a granola bar out of the cupboard in the kitchen and then walked out the front door.

She paused on the steps as a group of girls passed by. Of all the different types of humans, teenage girls were the closest to Kjin without actually being them. They were not evil, of course, they were just...well, mean. Not wanting to get caught up in the mean, Fallon avoided them at all costs.

She glanced over at the white house next door, grateful that Kade was nowhere in sight.

Fallon fell in behind the girls and joined the growing trail of young people making their way to Alden University. The school was only four blocks away, which was just as well since she did not have a car. Hoodie up and eyes averted, Fallon peeled off from the group when they reached the campus and headed to the registration office. There was a long row of students waiting to pick up their schedules, so she waited in line with them.

When she finally made it to the desk, she accepted the white paper from the clerk and was pleased to see *Forensic Science* typed across the top. At least Father Tomas did not sign her up for something way out of her comfort zone, like Engineering or Nursing. In order to have the access she needed at AU, she did have to play the part of a college student and, unfortunately, that included attending classes.

She had two that morning and hurried to the first one—Psychology.

The Professor was a portly gentleman who apparently saw himself more as a stand-up comedian than a teacher and spent most of the hour and a half telling jokes and inappropriately ribbing his returning students. The Professor of her second class, Biology, could have been speaking a foreign language for all Fallon understood a single word he said. Biology was definitely not for her.

She was a bit proud of herself, though, for managing to get through both without speaking a single word to anyone. She had become very skilled over the years at avoiding small talk and could head off a potential conversation with a single glare. Now that they were over, though, she had to find out where Professor Ellis' office was so she could start her surveillance and figure out a way to kill the monster.

She walked back toward the administration wing where she picked up her schedule that morning. The same woman was behind the desk.

Fallon put a smile on her face. "Hi. I am just wondering where I can find Professor Marc Ellis' office."

The woman raised her eyebrows. "Professor Ellis is not even teaching any classes this semester."

Fallon grimaced. This was not going well. She learned early on that it was best not to draw attention to herself when asking questions. It should be in and out. One question, one answer. No superfluous conversation. Unfortunately, it was too late now. She started to back away. "Never mind. I was just going to interview him—."

The woman snorted. "A project already?" She muttered something under her breath about demanding professors, and then returned her gaze to the papers on her desk. "Mr. Ellis' office is on the second floor of Bartlett Hall, but he's not there. He won't be in until Friday."

"Okay, thanks," she said and walked out of the office before the woman had time to remember her face. She headed for the exit.

Fallon did not hear his footsteps behind her, but smelled his spicy soap scent a few seconds before he clasped his hands around her waist.

She yelped. A high-pitched, girl yelp! One of the most powerful Knights of Emperica just yelped like a schoolgirl.

"What are you doing?" he asked her.

"I...I had to talk to the clerk." Since honesty was a virtue she embraced completely, she refused to lie. Even a white lie.

He took her hand and started to walk. "Come on."

She pulled back. "No, Kade, I can't...I have to..."

He turned to her, and she noticed that his eyes were rimmed red. "Look, I had some bad news today and just need someone to talk to."

"I wish I could, Kade."

"Ethan's dead."

She reached out and put her hand on his arm. "I'm so sorry. I don't know what else to say."

"Don't say anything. Just be with me. I need you."

This was crazy. She had to find out more about Professor Ellis. She had to find a way to stop this Kjin from hurting any more innocent people. Just this morning, she made the decision that she could not see Kade again.

"Please."

The pain in his voice touched her heart, and her mouth betrayed her head. "Okay," she said, and felt herself being pulled along by the force of Kade.

CHAPTER 6

The Guardian

"I wonder what happens when you die," Kade wondered aloud as he stared up at the sky with his hands behind his head.

"You go to heaven."

"Do you really think so?"

"I know so."

She saw the corners of his mouth twitch up in a wry grin. "I wish I could be so confident."

Fallon reached over and grabbed his hand. "Trust me. I have an inside connection with the big guy."

"Do you now?" He turned on his side and propped up on an elbow to look down at her. "I do know that I feel much better with you next to me. Thanks for being here. I didn't think you would come."

She laughed. "You really didn't give me much of a choice!"

He gave her a dimpled smile. "No, I didn't."

A hangout for college kids, they were lying together in the grass in a remote section of Highland Park adjacent to AU. They had been lying together for hours now getting to know each other.

She learned that Kade's parents lived locally, but he had been out on his own since he was eighteen. After a few minor jobs, he joined the local sheriff's department two years ago. For as long as he could remember, he wanted nothing more than to become a police offer, but since that part of his life was now over, his parents convinced him to enroll at AU. He had a younger sister named, Chelsea, and a dog named, Titus, and he spoke fondly of both. He talked about his friend, Ethan, and she laughed with him as he recalled some of their best childhood adventures and pranks.

Fallon let him do most of the talking and only divulged that she lost her parents and brother to a home invasion some years back and now lived by herself in Buffalo. She actually traveled all over the east coast in her efforts to track the Kjin, but her apartment in Buffalo was her primary residence. She did not call it *home*, because it wasn't. A home was a place of comfort and memories and love. Buffalo was a place to lay her head at night.

Due to the criminal nature of her loss, Kade's ears perked up. "A home invasion? Were the perpetrators ever caught?"

"No."

A look of sympathy filled his eyes. "I can't imagine how difficult that must have been for you. You were so young."

Every time she closed her eyes at night, the image of her brother's ruined body flared through her mind. "Yes, it was pretty hard."

"That's why I always wanted to be in law enforcement. To get scum like that off the street. I'm sorry you had to go through that." He reached out and rolled a piece of her hair between his fingers. "You are very beautiful," he commented huskily. "But, it is not just that. There is something special about you, Fallon. I don't know what it is."

She lowered her head shyly. "I'm just a girl, Kade, who likes a boy." *Really, Angell?* She would have to wear a muzzle if this kept up.

He reached out and lifted her chin so she had to look at him, and the desire that colored his handsome features was far from boyish. "Now, that is something I can get used to hearing," he murmured and lowered his lips to hers.

It was such a sweet, tender kiss, but one that ignited a fire raging through her body. More for the intimate emotional connection it forged between them than in physical need. He mouth moved slowly, but left her breathless with the promise it held. She never wanted him to stop.

"Help! Someone help me!"

Fallon jumped to her feet in a flash. Probably a little too fast if the look on Kade's face was any indication. She sprinted to the sound of the cries.

"Help! My daughter!"

A woman was waving her arms frantically at one of the scenic areas common in upstate New York that overlooked a fairly large gorge. Fallon rushed to the waist high stone wall where the woman was pointing. There, thirty feet below, a young child was crouched on the edge of a small protrusion in the cliff face.

The child's mother climbed over the wall, ready to try and rappel down, but the terror on her face was clearly evident.

Fallon grabbed the woman's arm before she fell, too. "No, let me. I have some skill in rock climbing."

The terrified woman hesitated, apparently not sure if she wanted to put the fate of her daughter in the hands of such a young girl. But, she did scramble back over the wall. "Are you sure? Can you save her?"

Fallon nodded. "I can."

Kade caught up to her. "Boy, you're fast. What's going on?"

"There's a little girl stuck in the gorge. I'm going to go down and get her." She ignored his look of disbelief. "Can you find a rope or something that I can tie around her waist? Then, you can pull her back up."

"What? No! You are not going over that wall! I'll go."

She shook her head. "No. I'll need your strength to pull us up after I get down there. Don't worry. I've done this before. Just get me the rope before that little girl falls."

Actually, she was not worried about the child in the least. She had already seen the glow of the guardian angel next to her.

Kade looked divided. He wanted to help the child, but was worried for her.

"Go!"

Her shout finally sent him moving, and he sprinted off with a frustrated growl.

With the mother safely back on this side of the wall, Fallon went over. It was a vertical descent, but she would have no problem. She could clamber down easily, but the real trick was in making it look like she did not have otherworldly abilities.

The guardian angel spoke to Fallon in her mind as she started her descent.

Hello, Knight.

Hello, Sentinel. Is the child all right?

Yes, she will not fall with me by her side.

What is her name?

Emma. The angel said the name with pride and love. *She is a curious little girl. I can see that I will have my hands very full with this one over the years.*

Fallon glanced down. It was maddening to have to proceed so slowly down the cliff face. *How is everything in Emperica, Sentinel?*

Soft tendrils of mist surrounded the angel's head as she smiled. *Glorious. How goes your fight here?*

Unending, Fallon said with a sigh.

Have faith in yourself, Knight, as we all have faith in you.

Fallon hurried down the last few feet and stepped onto the ledge, fighting back the tears at the Sentinel's words. This beautiful angel floating majestically in front of her was home. This was her family. And, she missed both desperately. But, it was not yet time to return. She still had work to do and all in Emperica were counting on her. *Thank you, Sentinel. Your presence alone has lifted my spirits.*

"Fallon! Here is the rope!" shouted Kade. "I have a few guys up here, and we will pull the child up once you tie it around her waist." The rope dropped down over the side of the embankment.

Fallon crouched in front of the girl. "Emma, my name is Fallon, and I don't want you to be afraid."

The little girl nodded.

"The men at the top are going to hoist you back up to your Mom, okay?"

Fallon grasped the rope and quickly constructed a sling for the little girl and had her step into the leg holes she created.

"Now, Emma, I want you to be a big girl and hang on tight. You're going to go for a fun ride back up to the top."

"Okay. I will."

Fallon called up to Kade. "All set! You can pull her up now." She watched as the little girl was carefully inched upward back toward her anxious mother.

I need to follow to make sure she does not fall. It was nice to see you, Knight. The angel lifted a hand to cup Fallon's face and it felt like the tickle of a warm, summer breeze.

Goodbye, Sentinel.

The lovely creature spread her wings wide and floated to the top after her charge.

A sharp pang of regret for the loss of her own wings wrenched Fallon's heart and instinctively she shrugged her shoulders. But, instead of the miracle of unfurling wings, it was only a dull ache that she felt now.

As soon as Emma was pulled to safety, Fallon scaled the cliff face.

Kade leaned over the wall. "Fallon, we are sending the rope back—"

Fallon poked her head up in front of him. "Already here!"

She wanted to laugh at the look on his face.

"How did you get up so fast? What are you? Some kind of spider?"

"Just your average superhuman teenager," she confessed truthfully.

He took her by the arm to help her over the wall. "Well, I'm pretty impressed with you, Fallon Angell. Not many people would have done what you just did for that little girl."

"I agree," said the mother, walking over to them. "I can't thank you enough. You don't know what you have given back to me. If there is anything I can do to repay you, let me know."

Fallon shook her head. "No, the sight of you and Emma together is payment enough."

The mother's eyebrows rose. "How did you know—?"

"Gotta go! Take care!" She pulled Kade's arm and they jogged from the scene as quickly as possible.

Kade stopped when they were far enough away from the scene of Fallon's heroics and took her in his arms. "See, I told you that there was something special about you. I just can't figure out if I am more impressed with you saving that little girl or the kiss you gave me right before."

She smiled, her cheeks hot. "You are a good friend, Kade Royce."

"Friend? Is that all?"

Her heart stopped. "What more would you like?"

"Everything. All of you. Every thought, every laugh, every hurt." He shook his head. "I can't figure it out either, but I am drawn to you in a way I have never been with anyone else."

She nodded. "I feel the same."

"My parents will be home tomorrow and have invited me to dinner. You're coming with me. And, I won't take no for an answer this time!"

She laughed inside her mind. When did he ever?

CHAPTER 7

An Encounter With Evil

"Forgive me Father, for I have sinned. It has been two days since my last confession."

"You are forgiven, child, although I doubt very much you have anything to be forgiven for."

"No."

"Report, please. Darius is anxious for news."

"Not much to report so far, Father. The Professor will not be at the university until Friday. Do you have a home address for him? Maybe I can track him down that way."

"Unfortunately, no. He moved recently and I do not as of yet have an updated address. Anthony is checking on that for me."

"Anthony?"

"My altar boy. Don't worry. He knows nothing except that I am trying to get the address of a parishioner."

"Then, I will come back tomorrow."

"Remember what I said, Fallon. A Knight has already been killed. You must find a way to catch him unaware."

"I will." She thought of something. "You said that this Kjin was taunting you. Why?"

The silhouette behind the screen tensed his shoulders. "I don't know. Perhaps he has found out somehow that I am an Emissier."

Fallon doubted that was the case. Unless Father Tomas himself divulged the information to the Kjin, there was no way for any of them to know that, as an Emissier, the priest was one of the select clergymen on earth who worked directly with Emperica and had access to the Elders.

"Maybe," she murmured noncommittally. "I will see you tomorrow, Father."

"Be careful."

Fallon stood and ducked out of the confessional. With her mind on her conversation with Father Tomas, she almost tripped over the altar boy scrubbing the floor just outside of the small compartment.

The boy reached up to steady her. "Oh, sorry! Are you all right?"

Fallon straightened. "Yes, I'm fine."

Red spots blossomed on the boy's face. "I didn't realize anyone was using the confessional."

"It's okay. Really. Are you Anthony?"

The young boy nodded, but looked at her suspiciously. "How do you know my name?"

"I'm Fallon, and a friend of Father Tomas. He mentioned you to me."

"Oh."

There was an awkward pause, and then she asked, "How old are you, Anthony?"

"I just turned sixteen," he said, glancing around nervously.

Fallon was surprised. He was small and looked to be no older than twelve. Not wanting to torment the obviously bashful young man any further, she nodded and walked past him. "Well, nice to meet you, Anthony."

"Okay. See you.

Just get me that address, Anthony, she thought to herself. *Nobody in this town will be safe again, until you get me that address.*

❧

Oh, where is Julian when I need him! Fallon stood looking at her meager selection of clothes to wear for dinner at Kade's house with a scowl. She needed to buy some new clothes, and soon. Then again, maybe she would not need them. After Father Tomas gave her the professor's address tomorrow, her stay in Alden could very well be over. The pretense of a college student at an end, she could then return to Buffalo.

The thought depressed her. What would she be going back to? A life of tracking Kjin, TV dinners, and solitude. Yes, that was her life and had been for four years now. So, why did it suddenly seem so unbearable? Kade Royce, that was why. Because thinking about leaving him behind made her physically ill.

She looked at the clock. He would be here any minute. Finally deciding on jeans, tee and a scarf, she walked down the stairs just as the doorbell rang.

Fighting back her nerves, she opened the door and could not help but smile at his dimpled grin. "Hi."

"Hi, Fallon. You look really nice."

She laughed. "Not true, but thanks for saying it."

He looked at her quizzically. "Of course it's true. Don't you have any mirrors in there?"

"I guess I just don't see what you see," she admitted.

"You're right. A mirror only reflects what is on the outside. As beautiful as that is," he said and reached out to stroke one side of her long hair, "it does not compare to what is inside of you. That is where you truly shine."

She smiled. "A romantic. And, how many girls have you said that to, Mr. Royce?"

His blue eyes smoldered. "Let's see. Counting you? Just one."

A warm flush rose in her face.

"Come on." He held his hand out to hers. "My family is going to love you."

She put her hand in his, and Kade led her down the steps to where his Jeep Wrangler was parked on the street. He held open the passenger door for her and as soon as she slid in, she inhaled the scent of Kade. The car reeked of his spicy soap scent and it was a comforting smell.

"Nervous?" he asked her when he got into the car.

She tried to still the butterflies in her stomach. "A little."

"Don't be."

Only two words, but she instantly felt more at ease.

It was a short ride to his parent's house, a well-kept brick Tudor, and as soon as Kade pulled into the driveway, a brown, Chesapeake Retriever loped up beside them with a loud bark.

"Titus, get back!" Kade yelled out of the window, but as soon as he got out of the car, he wrestled with the big dog affectionately.

Kade's mother waved from the front door, and his father rushed out to meet them.

The parents. The dog. The house. It was all so...normal.

Sudden, overwhelming longing surfaced in her mind. A single tear managed to get by her tightly held defenses, but she wiped it away in irritation and smiled for Kade's father.

He enveloped his son in a tight embrace. "It is so good to see you, son."

Kade patted his back. "Good to be home, Dad."

The two came apart and Mr. Royce smiled at her. "Welcome, Fallon. If you don't mind me saying, you are even prettier than Kade described."

"Dad!" Kade's cheeks turned scarlet.

"What? What did I say?" he asked with feigned innocence.

"Come on," Kade said with a glower and grabbed her hand.

Despite the scowl, it was all in good fun and the affection between father and son was obvious. The rapport warmed her heart.

"Hi, honey," Mrs. Kade greeted her son with tears in her eyes.

"Hi, Mom." Then, he turned to her. "Fallon, this is my Mom, Judy."

"Hello, Mrs. Royce, nice to meet you."

"You, too, sweetheart, now come on inside." Kade's mother held open the door, and Fallon stepped into a nicely decorated living room. The smell of cinnamon permeated the air. "Mmm. Smells delicious, Mrs. Royce."

"Oh, that's dessert. Kade just loves my homemade apple pie."

A shrill scream that started at the top of the stairs to the second floor and continued down in the form of a young girl, caused Fallon to laugh. The girl, who looked very much like Kade and could only be Chelsea, jumped over the last two bottom steps and threw herself into her brother's arms.

Kade caught her. "Chels! Relax. You just saw me three weeks ago."

The girl pouted. "Well, I haven't been able to hug you in way too long. I wanted to be there for you when you got out, but Mom and Dad *forced* me to go to Paris."

"Yeah, terrible aren't they?" Kade teased.

Chelsea laughed and Mrs. Royce snorted and disappeared into the kitchen.

Kade set her back on the ground and directed her gaze toward Fallon. "This is my friend, Fallon."

"Hi, Chelsea. Nice to meet you."

The feminine version of Kade raised her eyebrows. "Friend or girlfriend?"

"Give me another day and then ask again," Kade answered with a smirk."

Fallon punched him in the arm.

"Ouch!"

"You're very pretty," Chelsea commented to her.

Fallon blushed. "Thanks. You are, too."

Kade put his hand at the small of her back. "Come on, I want to show you my old room."

Fallon pulled back. "Won't your parents be upset?" she whispered.

He made a face. "Why would they?"

Fallon shook her head and let herself be pulled up the stairs. *Get a grip, Angell. This is a new millennium.*

Halfway up the stairs, Fallon nearly tripped when the Kur on her arm flared in a hot burn. A Kjin? Here?

She whipped her head around and glanced back down to the first floor. The front door was opening and a man stepped in, followed by a woman and four children.

"Hope we're not late."

"Uncle Marc is here!" Chelsea screamed to all within hearing distance.

"Marc?" Fallon hissed at Kade.

"Yeah, Marc Ellis. He's my uncle."

Fallon was stunned. The Kjin that had killed women and children was Kade's uncle? According to Father Tomas, he was also the one responsible for setting up his nephew on bogus charges that sent him to jail for an entire year.

It took more resolve than she thought she was capable of to suppress her anger and turn from the Kjin and continue to follow Kade up the stairs.

Shaking her head in regret, one thought filled her mind.

Why must she continue having to kill the people Kade loved?

CHAPTER 8

Caught in the Act

Distracted, Fallon glanced around at Kade's old bedroom. Apparently, nothing had changed since he last lived here.

"I still come and stay a lot," he said in response to her unspoken question.

It was a typical guy's room. Bed, laptop, and a fathead of Tony Romo gracing one wall. She turned to him. "Nice room—"

There was that yelp again! He grabbed her shoulders and pinned her against the door, snaking his knee between her legs to hold her in place. "What are you doing?" she croaked out.

The most amazing blue eyes she had ever seen stared down at her. "Looking at you." He lifted his hand and reached out to stroke her cheek. "Touching you."

Slowly, he leaned in and hovered his lips above hers. "Kissing you."

Her breath caught in her throat when he tipped her chin with his finger and their lips met.

This was so wrong, yet she was powerless to stop him. Her mortal enemy was downstairs at this very moment, and she was losing herself in a kiss. Enough! This had to stop.

But, he was the one to pull away. He shook his head and let go of her to sit on the edge of his bed. "What have you done to me, Fallon? If I didn't know better, I would say that you were a witch."

"Not quite," she murmured.

"What is it then?"

"Kade..."

He looked up at her with a sheepish smile. "I can't stand next to you and not be moved by you. Come on, Fallon, you saved a life yesterday with no regard to your own safety. How much more perfect can you be?"

"Kade..."

He held his hand out toward her. "Come here and kiss me, Fallon. Kiss me like you mean it."

She felt the same pull to him as he did to her. Her legs felt weak as she stumbled over to the bed and dropped to her knees before him. He reached out and framed her face with his hands, and when their lips touched again, she melted into him with a soft moan. Fallon's whole body tingled with desire, and she lost all abandon in his kiss. A low ache thudded through her lower body and she had to fight back the urge to cry out.

Embarrassed, she pulled away and sat back on her heels. When her courage returned, she lifted her head to look at Kade, and the depth of the naked emotion in his eyes floored her. Desire, compassion, innocence and, yes, the beginnings of love. Every feeling displayed in detail across his face was easy to read, because she knew they mirrored her own.

Sitting up again, she wrapped her arms around his neck and snuggled her face into the crook of his throat.

"Kade! Time for dinner!" Chelsea's yell up the stairs caused her to jump guiltily to her feet.

"It's okay," Kade assured her. "Nobody would come in here with my door shut."

Fallon was surprised. "Even with a teenage girl in here? Your parents are pretty liberal."

He shook his head. "No, they just trust me. Unfortunately, I don't trust myself very much right now." He stood and dragged her close to him once again. "We are together now, Fallon. Don't try to pull away anymore, okay?"

She nodded. It was all she could do.

"Let's go. I want you to meet my Uncle Marc. He's great, you'll love him."

Reluctantly, she followed behind him and was grateful that he did not seem to notice her hesitation. How could she explain to him that his uncle a vile demon? How long he had been so she did not know, but he had been killing women for a very long time.

Animated conversation drifted to her ears as they descended the stairs. Kade's parents, sister, and relatives were gathered around the television.

"Ssh! Listen," commanded Mrs. Royce.

The news was on and a pretty newscaster filled the screen. "Police have confirmed that there are still no leads in the disappearance of two local children. Six-year-old, Sammy Hutchinson, was last seen getting off the school bus three weeks ago, and seven-year-old, Carly Cox, went missing just last week from her own backyard. If anyone has any information regarding these two children, please contact Crime Control at the number displayed at the bottom of your screen."

An image of the children's crying parents came on next, and their heartfelt pleas were hard to listen to. Mrs. Royce walked over and turned off the television. "What a shame. Right here in Alden. It's just too shocking to contemplate. I can't imagine what those families are going through." She walked toward the kitchen. "If anybody has an appetite left, please sit down at the table. I'll be right out with the food."

"I'll help," said Chelsea.

Fallon glared at the Kjin. He looked very scholarly in his square glasses, sweater vest, and easy smile, but Fallon had to remind herself that it was not the outside that mattered, it was what lurked inside.

As everyone walked to the dining room, Mr. Royce suddenly remembered his new guest. "Oh, wait, you haven't met Kade's friend yet."

With difficulty, Fallon nodded politely to Marc Ellis and his wife, and then sat in the chair Kade held out for her. Her Kur was a painful flame this close to the Kjin.

She could feel Marc Ellis' eyes on her. "And, does this lovely creature have a name?" he leered.

His wife seemed indifferent to her husband's tone, but Kade was not. He threw a scowl at his uncle. "She's not a creature. Her name is Fallon. Fallon, this is my Uncle Marc, Aunt Ellie, and the four rug rats are Mia, Gino, Joey and Rachel."

After the greetings, Mrs. Royce returned from the kitchen with a platter of ham and relaxed conversation broke out around the table. Despite Marc Ellis' constant looks, Fallon enjoyed Kade's family. They were witty and smart and the conversation jumped from topic to topic.

After the dessert of apple pie, Marc Ellis scraped his chair back and declared to his family that it was time to leave.

With thoughts of the missing children still on her mind, Fallon did the same. She was not going to wait for Anthony to get her an address. She was going to get it herself.

"Thank you, Mr. and Mrs. Royce. It was a lovely dinner, but I must be going, too."

"Good night, Fallon. We hope you'll come back to visit again soon."

"I will."

Kade frowned. "Are you sure? I was hoping we could hang out for a little while yet."

She shook her head. "No, I really have to go. See you tomorrow at school, okay?"

He was clearly upset with her decision. "Wait. I'll drive you home."

"No, you said you were going to spend the night here. I'll be fine, really. See you tomorrow." She left him to say goodbye to his relatives and slipped out of the door.

Kade entered his bedroom and shut the door, irritation lodged in his chest. Why did Fallon leave so abruptly? As far as he could tell, she liked him as much as he did her, but something was holding her back. Was she having second thoughts because of his stint in jail? He never did explain to her that it was a set up. Would she believe him? Whatever it was that was bothering her, he was determined to find out. He wanted to know everything and more about Fallon Angell.

He thrust his fingers through his hair and sat on the bed, his thoughts drifting to Ethan. Selfishly, he wished his best friend was still here to talk to. Granted, Ethan did undergo a major personality change in the last few days of his life, but it was possible he had something going on in his life that Kade knew nothing about. He regretted now that he did not make more of an effort to find out what was going on with his friend. Even behind bars, he could have been there as a sounding board.

Downstairs, the front door slammed shut, and Kade stood from the bed and went to the window. His uncle, aunt and cousins were piling into their black Escalade.

Maybe he should go to Fallon. He really wanted to see her again. He was not lying when he said he felt a powerful connection to her. Even now, he was aching to be near her. Everything seemed drab and gray in comparison to the light of her presence.

As soon as the black SUV started down the street, he started to turn from the window, but a movement caught his eye. He peered back down onto the street. It was Fallon! And, she was running down the street after his relatives' vehicle. *What is going on here?*

He ran from his bedroom and then down the steps. "Mom! Dad! Be right back!"

Flying through the front door, he raced down the street. Neither Fallon nor the Escalade were in sight. Was Fallon really following his uncle and aunt? Maybe it just looked that way. The Ellis' moved into a new cul de sac a month ago about six blocks from his house, so he decided to head there to see what he could find out.

Pumping his arms and legs for three blocks, he finally caught sight of Fallon and the brake lights of the SUV. She kept close to the shadows of the sidewalk and slowed every time the Escalade came to a stop sign.

There was no question now. She was following them.

But, why?

Another vehicle approached. It was a green truck and it pulled up next to Fallon. A young man stuck his head out of the window of the driver's side. "Hey, beautiful. We're headed for a party. Why don't you come with us?"

"No, thanks," he heard Fallon mumble distractedly.

The car pulled to the curb. "Wait up!"

The man threw the truck in park and opened the door. From the way he stumbled over to Fallon, it was obvious that he had been drinking.

Fallon started to jog away from him, but he launched himself at her and took her to the ground.

Kade cursed under his breath, but before he could act, the drunk screamed out and went flying through the air. He landed flat on his back in the street with a loud grunt.

The passenger side of the truck opened and another guy got out and ran to his friend. "What did you just do to him?" he asked Fallon as she stood back up.

"Just leave," she told him.

"Not until you tell me what you did to him," he spit out.

"Nothing. Now go. Just get your friend out of here and no one will get hurt."

Kade could tell that the man was getting angry now. "What did you use on him? Some kind of taser?"

Fallon turned to leave and the guy jumped over his friend to push her. With lightning speed, she sidestepped out of the way and he stumbled by her. With a furious snarl, he turned and swung his arm to backhand Fallon, but she caught him by the wrist and twisted, pinning his arm behind his back. He cried out in pain.

"Didn't you ever learn that no means no?" she asked the guy with his arm still clutched firmly in one hand. With the other, she reached around to her back pocket and pulled out what looked like a knife.

Kade tensed, unable to believe what he was seeing. *Is she really going to stab the guy?* Kade took a step forward to intervene, but stopped when Fallon pushed her attacker away and slammed the hilt of the knife to the bracelet she wore on her bicep. He blinked in surprise when a glowing sword lit up the night.

Before the man could recover for another attack, she waved the weapon before his face, and his eyes glazed over.

Fallon hit the hilt of the blade of light to her bracelet once again, and the sword disappeared.

Too dazed to do or say anything, Kane could only watch in stunned silence as Fallon turned and ran from the scene. The young man stood immobile for a moment, but then shook his head in confusion. He glanced down at his friend lying on the ground as if trying to piece together what had happened.

Kade knew how he felt. He was trying to do the same thing.

Finally, the man reached down, helped his friend to his feet, and put him into the truck. With one last wary glance around, he jumped into the driver's side and sped down the street.

Kade turned and walked back toward his parents' house. He wanted to tell them that he would not be staying the night after all. No, he was going back to Oak Street and the yellow Victorian next door.

He was going back for answers.

CHAPTER 9

The Truth

If Fallon cursed, she would have done so then. She lost Marc Ellis' Cadillac and had no way of knowing where he went. She walked the streets for blocks but did not find it.

All because of a drunk. It had been risky to erase his friend's memory with her Aventi out on a public street, but he left her with no other choice when he witnessed her unnatural power. It always bothered her when she had to resort to memory tampering, preferring instead to avoid trouble in the first place. She could only assume how unnerving it must be for a person to have a fragment of time missing from their life.

Fallon started back toward Oak Street. Fortunately, all was not lost. She still had two other ways to get the Kjin's address. Either Father Tomas' altar boy would obtain it or, now that she knew about the Kjin's connection with Kade, she could get it from him. Surely, she could find a way to get the information without arousing too much suspicion. Either way, it would have to wait until tomorrow.

While she walked, she thought back to her visit to Kade's house and especially the few stolen moments in his bedroom. No one had ever looked at her the way he did and the feelings he stimulated in her were both thrilling and terrifying. She had known love before, of course. Her parents and brother. Friends. The supreme love of the Creator and the angels in Emperica. But, this was different. It was an emotion so strong that it felt like a natural part of her. Even now, she wanted nothing more than to run to him and back into his arms. She had this unexpected urge to make sure that he was safe and happy.

Feeling anxious now, she picked up her speed, grateful for the darkness that would help conceal her swift movement. She had to slow several times because of people on the streets, but soon her yellow Victorian came into view.

She stopped.

Someone was sitting on the front steps of her house. Cautiously, she approached and her heart fluttered in her chest when she recognized Kade. *He came home!* Grinning, she ran to him in excitement but pulled up short when he did not return the smile.

"What is it?" she asked, wondering if something had happened to one of his family members. "Is everything okay?" It was hard for her to read the odd expression on his face. "Kade, what's going on?"

He snorted. "You tell me."

"Tell you what?" Suddenly, a sinking feeling developed in the pit of her stomach.

"You can start by answering question number one, Fallon. Why were you following my relatives?"

She just stared at him. She refused to lie to him, but could not tell him the truth either.

Or could she?

"Well?" He stood up to face her. "Are they in some kind of trouble with the law?"

She turned her back to him.

"Are you some kind of agent or something? I saw you following them. I also saw you use some kind of weapon that completely messed up the guy that attacked you. I don't like secrets, Fallon, and I don't like to be lied to. Obviously, you are someone other than what you have told me."

This was why she never sought out entanglements with humans. She always feared that if she let people get too close to her, they would find out things they should not know. Her fears had been justified.

He put his hands on her shoulders. "Tell me. Who are you?"

"I...I can't."

"Tell me!"

"You wouldn't believe me."

"Fallon! Whatever it is, I can deal with it. I can deal with anything rather than lose you. Tell me!"

In that moment, she decided she would tell him. She *needed* to tell him. Four years was too long to go without companionship. Too long not to laugh or to share ideas or to feel the touch of another human being. She choked back a sob. Yes, she would tell him.

And, after you tell him everything about your life? What then, Fallon?

She would have to erase his memory, so he would never have any recollection of ever meeting her. The lump that formed in her throat made it hard to swallow. He did not understand what he was asking. He did not realize that if she told him the truth, it would cost them their relationship.

"Well, Fallon?" he interrupted. "What are you?"

Slowly, she turned to face him. "I'm an angel."

Inside the foyer to Fallon's house, Kade took her into his arms and held her close. With a deep breath, he inhaled the lavender fragrance of her hair. "Go upstairs," he told her, pulling away to hold her at arm's length. "I'll grab us some sodas."

She nodded woodenly and walked up the steps.

Kade hurried into the kitchen and the refrigerator. He did not want to leave her alone for long. It was obvious that she had some kind of breakdown, but he was not sure what caused it.

She called herself an angel. Did this word have another secret meaning or did she really think she was an *angel* angel. The kind with wings? He shrugged. Somehow, he had to get the truth out of her as gently as possible. Grabbing the sodas, he hurried up the stairs and found her bedroom. She was sitting on the wide bench seat at the window and looking down onto the street. At that moment, bathed in moonlight with her long, blonde hair flowing down her back, she really did look like an angel.

"Fallon? Are you okay?"

She nodded with a small smile, and he handed her the soda.

"You're scaring me," he admitted to her.

"I don't mean to."

"I know. As long as you're feeling okay, that's all that matters."

"I'm fine."

"Do you want to talk?"

"I don't think we have any other choice now."

He sat beside her and pulled his feet up to lean back against the wall. "About this angel thing..."

"I was telling you the truth. I am an angel."

"That's funny. I thought angels had halos and wings," he said with a soft laugh, trying to bring levity to the situation.

"My wings were clipped." She stood and turned her back to him. Crossing her hands in front of her, she grabbed the sides of her shirt and pulled it over her head.

He gasped, but was not sure if it was from the two long, angry scars just beneath her shoulder blades or for the fact that he was staring at her naked back. He felt both empathy and desire course through his body at the same time. "What happened?"

She swallowed. "I told you. My wings were clipped." She reached down, put the tee shirt back on, and sat again, drawing her knees up and facing him as she leaned against the opposite wall.

"So, you're really going with this angel thing?"

She smiled tiredly. "It's all I have."

Kade realized in that instance that she really believed it.

"You don't believe me," she whispered. "I can see it all over your face."

Was he that obvious? What did he think about this? He believed in heaven, certainly, and even angels. But they existed in another dimension, not here on earth. "I wouldn't say that. I'm just trying to figure out why you think the way you do."

"Because it's the truth."

"So, how did you get here on earth then?"

Slowly, Fallon told him an unbelievable story. How she and her family died thirty-four years earlier at the hands of two robbers. She talked about her journey to heaven, which she called Emperica, and training with the Knights. Julian, the boy she brought to his party, was also a Knight. She described the different castes within Emperica and why she chose the path she did. She told him about the evil Kjin that walked the earth in the form of humans and her mission to eradicate them from the world. Lastly, she discussed her return four years ago and all of her progress in fulfilling that obligation.

An hour later, Kade leaned his head back against the wall with a thud. The story was implausible. He knew that no sane person could hear the story Fallon just related and not think she was crazy.

He also knew something else.

She was wrong. He did believe her.

"So, that sword thing that you use. What does it do?"

"It's called an Aventi and it removes all memory of my existence. Want me to show you, Mr. Royce?"

He held his hands up. "No! I would like to keep my memories of you if that's all right."

A strange look passed over her face, but he was not sure why. Reaching his hand out, he touched the gold bracelet around her arm. "And, this?"

"It's an activator. It's called a Kur and brings the Aventi to life."

He stood up and speared a hand through his hair. "So, you basically run around and kill bad guys. All by yourself?"

"I'm hardly defenseless, Kade. I am strong. Much stronger than you."

He narrowed his eyes. "Hmm...I will have to test that out some time."

"Don't. I wouldn't want to hurt your male ego. I heard they were pretty fragile." Finally, a genuine smile from her.

"Mine more than most," he confessed. "How many others Knights are there?"

"On earth? A few hundred, but we hardly ever work together." She hesitated. "You actually knew one of the Knights."

"Who?"

"Gabe Mackey."

Kade reeled at the news, but immediately sorted back through his memories with Gabe and some things that seemed odd at the time started to make more sense. "Have you ever told anyone else about this?"

She snorted. "I don't think I have said more than ten words to another person in the last four years, let alone disclose this. I hope I don't have to tell you how important it is that you do not discuss with anyone else. Ever."

"Of course not. I would never betray you, Fallon, I promise you that."

She nodded.

"Who are you tracking now? Who is this Kjin person?"

She turned to the window. "I would rather not talk about that now. I'm really tired and I just want to lie down."

He went to her side and lifted her into his arms from the bench seat. She wrapped her arms around his neck, and he carried her to the bed and set her down gently.

For a long moment, he stared down at her and for the first time, she looked fragile to him. Not in a physical sense, but emotionally.

"Turn over."

He heard her soft intake of breath, but after a short hesitation, she rolled onto her stomach.

He sat beside her on the edge of the bed, lifted her shirt, and tenderly fingered the scars on her back. She flinched at the contact. "Don't." Her voice was tortured and husky.

"Why?"

"Because I'm embarrassed."

"Of what?"

"No one has ever seen my scars before."

"Did it hurt? When they clipped them?"

"Unbelievably so."

"I think they are incredibly beautiful."

"How could scars be beautiful?"

"Because they tell me what kind of woman you are. One who would endure such pain just to help others is very rare. You are really exceptional."

"It's quite obvious that you are the special one, Kade. I'm actually surprised you're still sitting here."

"I will never leave you, Fallon." He leaned down and tenderly kissed the back of her neck. When she turned to face him, he laid down alongside her and brushed his lips against hers, feather light. A low whimper escaped her throat, and the room began to spin with his heightened awareness of their bodies pressed so close together. His muscles tightened with need.

"Kade, I can't."

He sat up and let out a deep breath. "I'm sorry."

She put a hand on his arm. "You should know that I'm a virgin, Kade, and plan to remain that way."

"A virgin? Even before, you never...?"

"Never."

"And, you plan to remain a virgin until you're married?" he asked incredulously.

"Married?" she scoffed. "I don't think marriage is in the cards for me, Kade."

He did not laugh and his eyes narrowed in seriousness. "Oh, you will marry me one day soon, Fallon."

"Kade!"

He jumped off the bed and knelt, grabbing her hand in his. "I mean it. I love you, Fallon. I know it sounds crazy and impulsive, but I have never been more sure of anything in my life."

A lone tear made its trek down her face, but she did not respond.

Her silence gripped his heart. "Am I alone in how I feel, Fallon, or do you love me, too?"

She shook her head. "It wouldn't matter how I feel. I could never put you in the kind of danger that is my life."

"I can help protect you, Fallon! Your cause is now mine. We will fight together. Don't you want someone by your side? Someone to share your life?"

He could tell that his questions struck a chord with her when she began crying inconsolably.

"Don't answer me now," he whispered. "But, think about it, okay?" She was lying on top of the blanket, so he lifted one side and held it open. "Come on. Scoot in." Surprisingly, she heard him and lifted her body to snuggle under the covers. When he got into bed beside her, she did not protest. "Go to sleep now. I am watching over you, Fallon, tonight and for all the nights to come. You are not alone anymore."

CHAPTER 10

A Sinful Confession

Marc Ellis sat in his office at the university and watched through the windows as the students made their way to morning classes, his furious thoughts of Fallon Angell consuming him.

The girl knew, of course, what he was the moment he walked into his sister's house for dinner last night. Her Kur would have told her that.

He slammed his hand on the desk. What were the chances that his idiotic nephew would meet and bring home a Knight of Emperica! *The* Knight. The Knight he had been ordered by his superior to lure to Alden as she was responsible for the deaths of more Kjin in the past four years than any Knight in memory.

And, his plan worked. She was here and soon the means to dispose of her would arrive as well. His soldiers were assembling, and his associate at the church was seeing to the details at his end.

His only real concern was that the girl would disclose their true natures to his nephew. If she did that, he would be forced to leave Alden and start all over with a new body. He hoped to Tyras it did not come to that. He enjoyed his life here with money, prestige, and access to all of the beautiful young women he could get his hands on. No, he would not be pleased to have to begin again.

The more he thought about it, the more he became convinced that she would not say anything. She was bound by her angelic oath to keep humans safe and dragging Kade into this would only endanger his life. In the end, he decided she would most likely handle this on her own, and it would be her undoing.

He knew the Knights were under the mistaken belief that the Kjin were not organized, but they were. A new rigid hierarchy existed among their ranks, and he enjoyed a high position among his brethren, second only to his superior, a singularly ruthless Kjin, who had access to Tyras himself.

Since Tyras was powerless at the moment to send additional Kjin to earth, he made it clear to Marc's superior that he did not want to see a decrease in numbers before his plans could be put into motion. To that end, several Knights had been singled out and targeted for assassination.

Marc's orders were simple.

Kill Fallon Angell.

ꙮ

Fallon came awake slowly, reluctant to let go of her dream. Burrowing deeper into the sheets, she reached out and her hand found Kade. She smiled. It was not a dream after all.

She fought the urge to wrap her arms around him and snuggle into his back. He said he loved her. For a moment, she let herself believe that she could actually have a normal relationship with him. Why not? Impossible as it seemed, the biggest obstacle had already been overcome. He knew what she was. He knew, and he still wanted to be in her life.

She turned to gaze at him. His lips were parted slightly and his hair was tousled from sleep. He looked so innocent. So beautiful. It seemed like she had known him all her life instead of just a few days. He loved her, she thought once again in wonder. Although, most would call it rash and ridiculous, in the end, they were just words. Her heart did not care one bit about rashness, and her body's visceral response to Kade's touch was as far from ridiculous as one could get.

He murmured sleepily as she rose from the bed. "Fallon?"

"I'm here," she replied.

"Don't go."

"I'm just getting into the shower. We're late for classes."

He raised himself up on one elbow and the sheet fell down to his waist. He did not have a shirt on. *Wow, how has he been hiding those muscles?*

"How are you feeling?" he asked.

"Much better, thanks to you. I'm sorry about last night."

"I'm not. I found out that you're an angel and that I am hopelessly in love with you. Nope, not sorry at all."

She walked over to him and kissed him on the forehead. "Thank you."

He grabbed her arm. "Wait. I just thought of something. After what you told me last night, it's obvious that you're not really a college student."

She shook her head, trying to ignore the sight of his smooth, naked chest. "No, but it's still a cover I have to keep for now. You, on the other hand, *are* a college student, so get out of here and get ready. I'll meet you outside in about thirty minutes."

Reluctantly, he got out of bed, retrieved his shirt from the floor and pulled it over his head. She was grateful that he was still wearing his jeans. "Okay, I'll see you in a few."

As soon as he left, she went into the bathroom, turned on the shower and stepped into the hot spray. The thought of erasing her existence from Kade's memory weighed heavily on her, with that stubborn heart of hers warring against her mind for control.

Her heart was very convincing. What harm could there be in waiting a little longer? After all these years, why couldn't she enjoy this special connection she found with Kade. At least for a few more days. It was not like he would ever be in any real danger, right? She would make sure of that.

Her head was just as resolute. She was a Knight of Emperica for goodness sake. She had her duty, and the lives of countless people depended on her vigilance. Kade would never be safe in this world of hers.

In the end, her heart won. She would wait to erase his memory because anything else was unthinkable.

Feeling more at ease, she hurried through her shower, toweled herself off and dressed quickly. Not only did she have to suffer through two classes today, but she also had to see Father Tomas.

She grabbed her backpack and ran down the stairs. Kade was waiting for her out on the sidewalk in front of the house. He gave her a dimpled grin and kissed her chastely on the mouth when she approached. "It's been too long," he murmured.

She barked out a laugh. "Yes, a whole twenty-eight minutes."

"If felt like a lifetime to me."

Suddenly, the shrill sound of a siren cut through the early morning quiet. "Where is it coming from?" she asked.

"Just south of here. Come on."

Together, they ran the two blocks to Main Street. She looked west toward the highway that ran perpendicular and found the source of the siren. Fallon's heart lurched as she glimpsed two vehicles, crumpled and smoking from a fiery collision. But, even brighter than the fire was the glow of all the angels hovering over the accident scene. There were both Aegians and Sentinels, which meant that there were survivors as well as victims.

Fallon watched in fascination as the guardian angels flowed into the tight spaces of the cars and provided calming ministrations to the injured. She knew that was why most people never remembered the pain or exact details of the traumatic events in their lives. It was due to the protective force of their guardian angels and their caring, loving touches.

The sight was touching to witness, and Fallon's smile did not go unnoticed by Kade.

He put his hand on her arm. "Are there angels around those vehicles?" he asked.

She turned to face him in surprise. "Yes, but how do you know that? Can you see them?"

He shook his head. "No, but I can sense some kind of energy there. It is like an enormous halo of light surrounding the cars, and it's seriously making the hair on my body stand up straight."

Julian was right. Kade most certainly did have Intuit tendencies.

"Yes, the angels are there. Come on," she said softly and reached for him. "All of those people are in good hands."

They walked in silence to the university and said a quiet goodbye once inside.

Fallon tried very hard to listen in on her instructor's lessons, but it was difficult. Always eager to learn more, usually assignments like this were welcome. Now, though, she found herself distracted by Kade.

"What do you think, Ms. Angell?" The professor's voice startled her out of her musings, as it was meant to.

"Oh, sorry, can you repeat the question?" she asked, straightening in her chair.

He did and fortunately, she knew the answer. After that, the rest of the class and the one after went by agonizingly slow. As soon as her second class ended, she flew out of the doors and into the unseasonably warm weather. She was anxious to tell Father Tomas that she had met up with Marc Ellis. Most likely, Anthony had the Kjin's home address by now, but having already met Marc Ellis' wife and four children, she wanted to keep the confrontation with him as far away from them as possible. She already decided that tonight, she would take the fight to his office at the university. If he was there, all the better. She could end his reign of destruction once and for all. If the office was empty, at least she may be able to find some clue as to what he was planning next.

Arriving at the church, she climbed the stone steps, entered the dark interior, and immediately felt her anxiety slipping away. She hurried to the back pew for a short prayer and then stood and slipped into the confessional.

"Forgive me Father, for I have sinned. It has been one day since my last confession."

"You are forgiven, child, although I doubt very much you have anything to be forgiven for."

She paused and the silence hung in the air between them.

"Fallon?"

"Sorry, Father. Yes, I think I do need to seek forgiveness."

"What is it, child?"

"I find myself very attracted to a man I met." She would not confess to him yet about her disclosure to Kade about her true identity. She was not ready to share that bit of news.

"Do you have strong feelings for him?"

"Very much so."

He chuckled softly. "I see. Desire and love are not sins, Fallon."

"But, I am an angel, Father! A fifty-year-old angel!"

"On this earth, you are still a teenager, Fallon. Raging hormones and all."

"But, I'm not even human."

"Of course you are. You are a human who has been on a great journey and back again, yes. A human with supernatural strength and otherworldly knowledge, yes, but a human nonetheless. You are not immortal. Although it would be extremely difficult to do, you can be killed."

When she remained quiet in contemplation, he continued.

"Fallon, love is not denied to you. Love is one of the greatest gifts the Creator has bestowed on us, and there is nothing more precious than sharing your love with others. A world without love, is a world without light. Corinthians 13:13, Fallon. 'And now these three remain: faith, hope and love. But the greatest of these is love.' You would do well to remember that."

❧

Fallon exited the confessional with a lighter heart. Father Tomas was right. Love was the most precious of all gifts, and she would not deny its existence in her life any longer.

Turning the corner of the aisle that ran along the back corridor of the church, she ran into the altar boy, Anthony.

The boy squealed when he saw her and dropped the papers in his hands.

"Anthony, what is wrong?" she asked, bending to help him pick them up. Why did he always seem so nervous around her?

"Nothing. You just startled me is all."

"Are you okay? You seem jumpy about something."

His eyes hardened. "I guess I am a little jumpy. I found..." He cut off what he was about to say.

"Found what?" she prompted, but he closed down again.

"Nothing. Where is Father Tomas?" he asked and his wide eyes quickly searched the church interior.

He seems afraid of something. But, what? "Father Tomas went back to his office," she informed him and handed the last paper to him.

The boy visibly relaxed.

"Look, Anthony, I know we hardly know each other, but I'm here if you want to talk about anything."

The boy shook his head. "No, it's nothing. I have to go." With that, he turned and fled out of the front doors of the church. As soon as they closed behind him, she noticed that he had left one paper on the ground. She immediately picked it up and rushed out, but he was already running as fast as he could away from the church. With a shrug, she put the paper in her pack, deciding she would return it to him tomorrow.

The sun that greeted her outside was a bright, yellow ball in the sky and its presence brought out a crowd of people to bask in the unexpected warmth. As Fallon walked among them, she recalled her conversation with Father Tomas with a smile. But, although she was ready to invite Kade into her life, she refused to involve him in Knight business. The less he knew, the safer he would be until it was all over. Especially when *all over* meant that his uncle would be dead.

"Hello, beautiful."

She yelped when the voice in her ear developed hands that wrapped around her waist.

"Kade!"

"Boy, for a tough warrior Knight, you're awfully skittish."

Oh, yeah? In one smooth move, she reached behind her head and flipped him across her back and onto the ground in front of her. She dropped down and rammed her knee into his throat. "You were saying?"

He laughed. "Okay, you made your point, but let me up! There are people watching us."

She grinned and stood.

Red-faced, he smiled in humor at the snickers coming from the crowd, took hold of her elbow, and steered her away. "You *are* strong," he whispered. "Remind me not to mess with you again."

His comment bothered her. "If you're looking for the damsel in distress who needs a big strong guy to look after her, that's not me, Kade."

"Thank goodness!" He stopped and turned her toward him. "I fell in love with *you*, Fallon, and I love every single thing about you." He glanced around. "But, I will admit that I'm not sure if my ego can handle you flipping me on my back in public all the time."

She pursed her lips at him playfully. "You will just have to stay on my good side then."

"Well, that should be easy since all of your sides are good."

With a smile, she pulled his face toward her and he gave her an oh, so, sweet kiss.

"Mmm...the lips of an angel. I love you, Fallon Angell."

"I love you, too, Kade Royce." There she said it! Right on Main Street, Alden, in the bright afternoon as people walked all around them. She would not deny the gift in front of her any longer.

Throwing an arm around her shoulder, he said, "Come on. I have a surprise for you."

"A surprise?"

"Yes. You don't have plans for tonight, do you?"

Besides going to AU to break into his uncle's office? No. And, she could always do that *after* Kade's mysterious surprise. She was very anxious to find out what it was and to spend more time with him. "What do you have in mind?"

He tilted his head at her. "Don't you know what the word *surprise* means?"

She growled at him, but he ignored her and took her hand. "I have some papers to finish for school. I'll walk you home and then pick you up around eight. Okay?"

She nodded. "What do I wear?"

The glint in his eye said it all. "Very little."

Chapter 11

The Lake

A bathing suit? At night? Really, Kade? Thankfully, the warmth of the day held and the humidity was still high, draping over the town like a shroud.

She did not know where they were going, but he told her to wear a bathing suit under her clothes. Remembering that she did not even own one, she hurried out to a boutique on Main Street that afternoon. The choices were overwhelming, but relying on the clerk's advice, she finally chose a white bikini and hurried home.

Now, as she studied her reflection in front of the mirror, she was having regrets. She realized that nobody in her life had ever seen her in so little clothes. Her body was thin and toned from her constant workouts so she guessed she looked all right in it, but the top seemed too small to hold in her full breasts. She knew this style was what the other girls wore, but she felt so exposed. When all of her attempts to stretch the material over her bosom failed, she sighed and threw on her tee-shirt. Hopefully, it would be dark enough that nobody would notice.

When Kade knocked a few minutes after eight, she opened the door and his smile sent shivers racing through her body.

"You ready?"

"I guess. Will you tell me now where we're going?"

"Where all college kids go on a Wednesday night. A party at the lake. There will be swimming, a bonfire, dancing."

Disappointment surged through her. She was hoping to spend time with Kade alone. "A party? Kade, I'm really not good in social situations."

"Why not? You're smart, funny, beautiful."

She turned from him. "I don't know. I'm just not that comfortable. I never know what to say and usually end up saying something ridiculously embarrassing."

He scoffed at her. "I doubt that." Turning her by the shoulders, he lifted her chin so she had to look at him. "Look, I haven't had a chance to laugh or just hang out with people my own age in a long time, and I doubt you have either. Even Knights need to have fun once in a while."

She frowned at him. "You make it pretty hard for a girl to say no."

"Then, don't."

"Fine." And, if she sounded petulant, that was just too bad.

He pointed to his face as they walked outside. "It's the dimples, isn't it? Am I right?"

She laughed. "Yes, it is the dimples."

As before, he held open the door of his Jeep Wrangler and she got in.

"What lake?" she asked him when he slipped in behind the wheel.

"Rushden Lake. It's only a few miles from here." He reached over and squeezed her hand. "Stop being so nervous. It's a party, Fallon, not an execution."

Not wanting to put a damper on his first night out in a year, she smiled at him. "I'll try."

Enrique Iglasias came on the radio with *Tonight I'm Loving You* and the sexy lyrics filled the car as they drove to the lake. Kade continued to hold her hand and kept glancing at her with heat in his eyes.

"Stop it."

The innocent look was back. "What? I *am* loving you tonight."

"Just tonight?" she teased.

"Always."

"Keep your eyes on the road, Royce."

He laughed and sang along to the song, and she found herself singing with him.

After a short drive, they arrived at the lake, and Kade parked his Jeep among the other cars on a rise that overlooked the beach. There must have been at least fifty people down on the sand either standing and talking around a bonfire or swimming in the lake.

"Is it legal to have a bonfire on the beach?" she asked.

He shook his head. "No, but this is private property owned by Cody Harlen's parents. Cody goes to AU and hosts a bonfire every Wednesday night. But, since this is his last year at school, they probably won't be going on much longer."

Nervously, Fallon picked up her bag, got out of the car and followed Kade down to the shore.

"Officer Royce!" A guy with blonde hair and boyish good looks ran up to them.

"Just Kade, Cody."

"Oh, right. Hey, dude, none of us ever believed those charges against you. I just want you to know that."

Even in the growing darkness, Fallon could see that Kade was embarrassed by Cody's words.

"Thanks, I appreciate that." He turned toward her. "This is my girlfriend, Fallon."

Fallon's stomach clenched with pleasure. She had never been a girlfriend before. She dated one boy in her old life, but it was not anything serious.

"Hey, Fallon, nice to meet you. Make yourselves at home. There's plenty to eat and drink so have fun."

"Thanks." Kade turned back to her. "Let's get something to eat and then go for a swim."

She nodded and found herself relaxing with Kade by her side. He reminded her of Julian with his easy wit and humor. They soon had a group of people around them and Fallon found herself laughing and enjoying everyone's company.

An hour later, Kade said, "Come on," and dragged her away from the crowd.

He led her to an isolated spot down the beach and pulled her down into the sand. With a dimpled grin, he leaned over and kissed her. "I have wanted to do that all night," he murmured against her mouth.

"Me, too," she admitted.

A full five minutes later, he lifted his head and asked her if she was up for a swim. When she nodded, he stood, helped her back to her feet and then shrugged out of his shirt.

Suddenly, feeling awkward, she set her bag on the sand. *Now that I think about it, there was a perfectly nice one-piece I could have bought!* With a shake of her head, she pulled her shorts down and stepped out of them. Finally, she pulled her shirt over her head.

She did not look up, but could feel Kade's eyes on her body. Without a word, he reached for her hand and led her to the water's edge. He let her get used to the temperature and then pulled her in deeper. When he put his hands on her waist and lifted her, she wrapped her legs and arms around him. It felt so intimate to be this close to him in the moonlight with the water lapping against their bodies.

"Kiss me," he whispered.

She did. With all of the passion and love she was feeling for the man holding her.

They kissed for several moments before he pulled away with a groan. "I don't think I can take much more than that. I am not the saint you are, Fallon," he confessed ruefully.

"I am not a saint, Kade."

"But—"

"Yes, there is a but, and you know what it is."

"Then, marry me."

She laughed. "You have asked me to marry you twice now and both times you were consumed with lust when you did."

He looked up to the sky. "Oh, I do lust for you, Fallon Angell. Very, very much." Dropping his gaze back down to her, he said, "But, I would take a lifetime of celibacy just to have you in my life."

Her heart melted with his words and she caressed his face tenderly. "Ask me to marry you again when your tongue is not hanging out."

"I think that can be arranged. Now, let's get out of here and get dressed."

Jumping free from his arms, she said, "Race you!"

She dove into the water and swam powerfully back to the shore.

"Hey!"

She heard him laugh as he tried to keep up, but he was no match for her.

When he made it on shore, he playfully tackled her and they fell to the sand in a giggling fit.

Fallon stiffened when she heard a rustle in the reeds lining the beach behind them.

"So, what do we have here?" said a menacing voice.

She leapt to her feet, followed quickly by Kade.

Two men with greasy hair and leather jackets stood looking at them.

Kade laughed. "Oh, this is going to be good. Gentlemen, you do not know what you're getting yourselves into."

Fallon did not laugh. "These are no gentlemen, Kade. They are Kjin."

❧

"Stand back, Kade," Fallon said, her tone deceptively soft as she dropped into a crouch.

"That's going to be a little tough for me to do, Fallon. You know that whole male ego thing you pointed out earlier."

She did not turn to him. "I mean it. Stay out of it."

"But, they're just human, right? No extra powers?"

She did not get a chance to answer when one of the Kjin took a swing at her head. She easily ducked underneath it and then jumped in the air to land a kick that hit him square in the chest, sending him flying back onto the sand.

The other Kjin did not hesitate. He rammed into her side and slammed her into the sand. She kept her knees up underneath his body as they fell and used the power in her legs to launch him into the air.

"Fallon!" she heard Kade shout out in warning.

The first Kjin stalked toward her again and tried to kick her in the ribs, but she rolled out of the way and vaulted back to her feet. He came at her fast with both fists flashing at her, but she jerked her head out of the way each time. Closing with him, she smashed the heel of her hand into his nose and heard the satisfying crunch of bone.

"Kade! My Aventi!"

"Where?" He sounded panicked.

"In my bag."

The second Kjin came at her, and she pummeled him with three quick jabs to the jaw and then landed a punch to the abdomen. He doubled over in pain.

"Here!" Kade screamed out and she turned to catch the Aventi he threw her way. Immediately, she banged it against the Kur on her arm and it flared to life.

The second Kjin cursed and ran down the beach still holding his stomach.

"Stay here!" she screamed at Kade. "When I release the shade with the Aventi, it will try to seek out another body. I don't want you anywhere near it!"

She took off at a run and was upon the fleeing Kjin in just a few seconds. She kicked him in the back and sent him sprawling in the sand. She stabbed him with one quick thrust of the sword and the demon wraith exploded out of the body, hissing in anger. Thinking only of her need to protect Kade, she pierced it a second time, and it disintegrated into black ash and drifted down onto the beach.

She rushed back to the first Kjin kneeling in the sand with his hands cupping his broken nose. She grabbed his hair and held the Aventi to his throat. "What are you doing here?" she snarled.

"Oh, just out for a moonlight stroll, darlin'," he said sarcastically, his voice already altered by the swelling on his face.

"I don't get it," Fallon said. "Why are you working together with another Kjin?"

"I do as I'm told," he drawled.

"So, you're taking orders from someone else. Who?"

"The blackcoat boss, darlin'." He turned his head toward Kade and lifted his lips in a bloody smile. "But, it's him that I'm interested in now. Come here, boy. You look like you have a strong body, and I'll be needin' one momentarily."

"Kade, go."

"Fallon..."

She never took her eyes off the Kjin. "Go!"

"I'll be waiting by the fire," he said reluctantly and walked away.

The Kjin tried to catch her off guard and lunge at her, but her Aventi slipped into his neck with ease. As soon as the dark specter rose into the night, she slashed it in two.

"That body is off limits to you, Kjin," she said softly into the night. "That one is all mine."

CHAPTER 12

All in a Knight's Work

They drove home in silence. Her brooding centered on trying to figure out why the Kjin seemed to be gathering in Alden. There was Marc Ellis, the man she killed when she first came to town, the Kjin who took possession of Kade's friend, Ethan, and now these two tonight. She could no longer deny that something was going on. The Kjin admitted as much when he said he was summoned by the blackcoat, whatever that meant. She decided to call a council with the other Knights in the area to see if together they could figure this out.

But, what was Kade brooding about? Was he put off by watching the violence of her actions tonight?

He pulled the Jeep up in front of her house, and she looked at his profile in the darkness. "What's the matter?" she asked him.

He grunted. "I'm a guy's guy, Fallon, and I think it's just going to take me some time to accept the fact that my girlfriend is stronger than I am."

She winced. "That ego again?"

"Yeah. It pretty much defines me."

"Ouch. Sorry."

He turned to look at her. "Don't be. It's who you are and I accept that. It just might take me a little time here."

"Do you want to come in?" She really should not even ask, because she needed to get to the university tonight to deal with his uncle, but she did not want to leave like this with his feelings so obviously conflicted about her. It felt unresolved.

"Can't. I have to get some sleep. Test in the morning."

"Okay, see you tomorrow." She reached over and gave him a kiss on the cheek.

"Good night," he whispered.

Why did it feel like he was really saying *goodbye*?

She stepped out of the car and, ever the gentleman, he waited until she went into the house and shut the door before backing up and pulling into his own driveway next door.

Hurrying up the stairs, Fallon stripped off her clothes and damp bathing suit. She chose black jeans and a black shirt and then retrieved her Aventi from her bag. Quickly tying her hair in a ponytail while she moved, she ran down the stairs and back out into the night.

The streets were quiet, and as she walked the four blocks to AU, her thoughts drifted to the events of this evening. For the first time since admitting to Kade that she was an angel, she was having second thoughts. It was too much too soon, and he freaked out. How could she expect a normal guy to accept and understand the paranormal? The thought that she may lose Kade brought a stinging burn to her throat, but she refused to allow any tears to fall. Tonight she had a job to do. The tears would have to wait.

She found the bricked, four-story Bartlett Hall in the administrative section of the campus. She knew the doors would be locked at this hour, so she slipped around the west side of the building, which was furthest from the road.

Stepping back to examine the exterior wall, she noticed one window on the third floor slightly ajar. That was all she needed. There would be enough handholds in the brick and mortar to make it to the window. Enough for her anyway. With one quick glance to make sure no one was around, she leapt at the building and began to scale the wall, shimmying effortlessly over the surface.

When she reached the window, she used her strength to pry open the window all the way and slipped inside. Soundlessly, she dropped to the floor.

The room was empty. It was a conference room of some sort and she hurried through it and out into the hallway. The clerk she spoke to on Monday told her that

Marc Ellis' office was on the second floor, so she found the stairs at the end of the corridor and started down.

The faint sound of a running vacuum cleaner from somewhere deeper in the building drifted to her, but it was too far away to give her serious concern.

Jogging down the hall, she looked at both sides of the corridor for nameplates or signs. Some doors had no labels, but she ran past them, deciding to come back only if she could not find the professor's office. But, she did find it. On a thick oak door at the end of the hall was the name Marc Ellis, President and Professor of Anthropology.

As she suspected, it was locked.

She slammed the heel of her hand into the knob, and the splinter of wood echoed in the hallway as it popped free of its casing. She pushed inside and closed the door behind her.

Moonlight streamed in the south wall made up almost entirely of glass. She moved to the enormous desk in the center of the room and began opening the large lower drawers. They were empty! How could they be empty? No files? No paperwork? Finally, she opened the narrow center drawer. There was a single piece of paper inside.

She took it out and unfolded it. It read, *Good evening, Miss Angell. I hope you will not be too disappointed that your search has turned up nothing. Thank you, my dear, for making my job easy. Goodbye, Fallon.*

Her blood ran cold.

Marc Ellis knew who and what she was.

As soon as she slammed the drawer shut, she heard a metallic click and every instinct in her body warned her that she set off a trip wire of some sort. She started to sprint to the door, but a blinding light stopped her in her tracks an instant before a thunderous explosion sent her sailing backwards out of the glass wall and into the night beyond.

∽

Fallon knew immediately that her back and legs were broken. She lay unmoving in the flickering glow and intense heat of the fire for several long moments before regaining the capacity to move. Fighting through the pain, she used the strength in her forearms to drag her battered body into the sculpted hedges that ringed Alden University. As loud sirens pierced the night and emergency personnel converged on the scene, she covered herself as best she could with leaves and branches from the ground. It would take some time for her injuries to heal, and she just hoped to remain hidden until then.

She did not have the energy to think about Marc Ellis or question how he could have known that she was a Knight. She would unravel the pieces later, after her health was restored.

For hours, she listened to the firemen fight the blaze as her body healed itself, realigning bones and knitting sinew back together. She felt every wrench as her fractured vertebrae fused back together. Sweat dripped from her brow and it took every bit of willpower she possessed not to cry out as she silently endured the agony caused by the healing and from being immobile on the cold ground for so long.

She had never been this hurt before and passed out twice during the night from the extent of effort needed to repair her injuries. Several times, men drifted close to her place of concealment in their search for evidence, but passed by without discovering her.

Only when the faint blushes of pink from the rising sun made their appearance, did she finally feel whole again. Tentatively, she tested the movement in her limbs and discovered that she was able to do so without pain.

Relived, she lifted herself into a squat and peered through the bushes. People were still mingling around the scene—mostly officers from the Alden CSI Team. Brushing the grassy debris from her hair and body, she exited the back of the hedge row and made the short walk back to her house unseen.

Without showering, she fell into her bed and drifted off to sleep with the knowledge that there would be no classes at AU today. Not that she would have attended anyway. That ruse was now over.

When she awoke again at ten o'clock, she felt better but was famished from the healing process. She went downstairs to make herself a breakfast of eggs and toast and after she ate, went back upstairs to take that much needed hot shower. As the water poured over her body, her mind focused on Marc Ellis.

He tried to kill her.

The note he left for her clearly indicated that the bomb was meant for her. How did he know she was a Knight? The more she thought about it, the more she realized that there was only one possible way.

Kade must have told him.

She shook her head in denial. It was impossible for her to believe. She trusted Kade. She trusted him with her life and no matter what the circumstantial evidence, she refused to believe he would betray her.

But, where was he?

He must have heard about the explosion last night. Surely, he would have wanted to check to make sure she was all right. Or, did he decide after seeing her destroy the two Kjin at the lake that he could not accept her for what she was? Was that what made him run to his uncle and tell him all he knew?

Earlier she had fell victim to Father Tomas' romantic notion that love was an option for her, but she had been a fool. That much was clear now.

Frustrated with herself, she turned off the shower and stomped out of the bathroom, dripping water over the floors. As she dressed, she ignored the pain in her chest and decided on her next course of action.

She still needed to get to Marc Ellis. To do that, she needed his home address if only to track his movements. Now that Kade was gone, that left Father Tomas' altar boy, Anthony. She would go to see him this morning.

Thinking of Anthony, she picked up her backpack and opened it. Inside was the paper the boy dropped yesterday. She took it out. It was a copy of an old newspaper clipping. Curious, she read through it carefully and grew more stunned with every word.

Father Tomas was arrested fifteen years ago for the murder of six-year-old Lilly Segal. Father Tomas? Why did he not tell her? He brought her to town to investigate the disappearance of two children in Alden without ever disclosing the fact that he himself had been suspected of killing one? Was this why Anthony had been so nervous? Was the boy afraid of Father Tomas?

Crumpling the article in her hand, she realized that she needed answers. Deciding to try the local library first, she grabbed her backpack and headed outside. Once out on the front steps, she could not help herself and glanced over at Kade's house, but everything was quiet and nobody appeared to be awake yet.

Oh, Kade, I am so sorry I cannot be the girl you need, because in truth, you are everything that I need.

She stepped off the porch and headed toward Main Street. The library was a block south of AU, so Fallon had to pass by the site of the explosion. She gasped when she saw the Sentinels and two new angels hovering over the still smoldering wreckage.

Then, she remembered.

The vacuum cleaner.

People had been in the building last night when the bomb meant to kill her detonated.

I will get you, Marc Ellis. You may know who I am now, but I also know you, and I promise that you will not get away with your evil for long. I'm coming for you.

With renewed determination, she walked the rest of the way to the library and entered the quiet interior. The clerk directed her to the row of computers that were set aside for public use. Selecting one, she sat down and entered Father Tomas' name and the word *murder*. The article from The Alden Press she already read came up as well as an account of the trial or, lack of trial, rather. The small town had been geared up for the proceedings and, at the last minute, the charges were dropped and Father Tomas was released from custody.

Most in town simply accepted the fact that their beloved priest was innocent. However, the family of Lilly Segal, the murdered child, was very vocal for many months regarding the injustice in this case. Eventually, though, all of the gossip faded away, and Fallon could not find a single mention in subsequent years. It was as if the incident had never happened.

She found it difficult to believe that an Emissier of Emperica was capable of murdering a child, but his omission was suspect.

Next, she typed in the word blackcoat. She had never heard of this word before the Kjin used it. The definition appeared on the screen as *n. 1. Black'coat, a clergyman.*

Clergyman? The Kjin said he following the orders of the blackcoat boss. So, that meant he was taking orders from a clergyman?

The certainty burgeoned unbidden in her mind. The Kjin was ordered to attack her by Father Tomas.

Feeling sick, Fallon left the library and wearily made her way back to her house. When she turned on Oak Street, she wished desperately to see Kade or his Jeep, but neither were home. The day could really not get any worse. She spent the morning healing broken bones, discovered that an Emissier was collaborating with the Kjin, and now another painful truth. Kade had left her.

She would need to speak to him at some point to warn him of his uncle. She had originally hoped to be able to take care of the situation quickly without him ever finding out the truth, but events had taken an ominous and more urgent tone and he was in danger. So, was his family. Fallon thought about his parents and sister, Chelsea. A Kjin, no matter what the relationship to the humans involved, would not hesitate to harm them if he or she thought it would be of benefit. It was in their nature.

Fallon entered her empty, cold house, and a pervasive sadness settled over her shoulders. *What is your problem, Angell? You have walked into empty houses for years. You should be used to it by now.*

She was used to it and that was the problem. Now that she had experienced the essence of true love for the first time, she did not want to let it go.

Lurching up the stairs in exhaustion, she peeled off her jeans, climbed into bed, and did something very unwarrior-like. She cried herself to sleep.

CHAPTER 13

Conditions

Kade sat in the dark and watched the soft and even flow of Fallon's breathing as she slept. She was so beautiful his heart ached just looking at her. But, there were tears on her cheeks. Why? He hoped nothing had happened to her while he had been occupied with his family last night. By now, she must have heard about the explosion at AU. His Uncle Marc had been devastated over the death of two custodians who were in the building at the time, so as soon as his mother called him that morning, the family gathered together at the Ellis home. As the day progressed, he found himself stuck there by the multitude of visitors that stopped by and the reporters camped out on the front lawn. This was big news not only for Alden but nationwide.

It was late when he returned home and while he did not intend to wake Fallon, he had to see her. He had to make sure that she was okay.

He snorted in his head. Who was he kidding? She did not need him for protection. She proved last night that she was more than capable of protecting herself.

Kade shifted in his chair and it made a small creaking noise. He was surprised that she did not awaken. Her angel instincts should have warned her that he was here. As soon as he had the thought, Fallon's slumberous breathing stopped, and in the next instant he was flat on his back with her Aventi at his throat.

"It's just me," he told her softly.

With a sigh, her body relaxed and she stepped away from him, walked to the edge of the bed and sat. He swallowed. She was wearing nothing but a tee-shirt and panties.

"Don't ever do that again," she scolded him.

Amused, he said, "That's twice now you've had me on my back. If I didn't know better..." The pain in her green eyes stopped him and he got to his feet. "What is it, Fallon?"

"I thought you left me," she whispered.

He walked over and stood before her. "I would never leave you," he said, truthfully.

She did not look convinced.

"But, I do have two conditions if we're going to continue this relationship," he told her.

"Conditions?" she asked with incredulity.

"Yes, number one. I will *never* stand back and watch you fight the Kjin without getting involved. Don't ever ask me to stay out of it again, Fallon. I'm not cut from that cloth, and it nearly killed me to walk away at the lake. You may be stronger than me, but I'm stronger than most of them, and I know how to fight."

Wait. Was that a small smile on her face?

"I think I can deal with that," she responded. "And, the second condition?"

"For the love of God, Fallon Angell, please don't ever, and I mean *ever*, fight like that wearing a white bikini again. I'm a man. Flawed as I am, there is only so much I can take. Promise?"

She shook her head. "I'll try. Now, you tell me, Kade Royce. Where have you been?"

He explained to her about his family get-together and his inability to get away. As each word passed his lips, he noticed that she grew noticeably more relieved. He knelt in front of her. Reaching out, he tilted her head up with two fingers under her chin. "You really thought I left you?"

"Yes."

"And, you're still mad at me, aren't you?"

She jerked her face away from his grip. "Yes, and I'm trying to play hard to get here, because I heard that's what girls are supposed to do."

He wanted to laugh, but figured that would probably not be a good idea right now. "Fallon, you are definitely not most girls."

"No," she agreed.

Her reaction confused him. "Did something happen that I'm not aware of?" he asked. "You heard about the explosion at AU, right?"

She shrugged and turned her head. "I was there."

"There? Where?"

She hesitated. "In your uncle's office."

"In his office?"

"Yes, Kade! I was in the office when the bomb went off. The power of the blast threw me out of the windows."

"What? Are you hurt?" He started to run his fingers over her body, but she pushed him away.

"It took awhile for me to heal, but I'm fine now. Exhausted, but fine."

That was why she did not hear him come in. He took her in his arms. "I'm so sorry, baby, that I wasn't there for you. You *should* be mad at me."

She sighed. "No, I shouldn't. I've been working alone for years. I don't expect you to get involved."

"But, I am involved now, Fallon. You have to accept that. You agreed to my conditions, remember?"

She gave him another one of her small smiles and nodded.

"Tell me. Why were you in my uncle's office?"

She scooted away from him on the bed and drew her knees up close to her body. "You may find it difficult to believe."

"Trust me. I would believe just about anything at this point."

"There is no easy way to tell you this, Kade, but the person you call your Uncle Marc, is actually a Kjin."

Kade stood and pulled away from her. "No...no, it can't be. I think I would know if my uncle was an evil demon, Fallon."

"He is."

"How can you be sure?"

"Many ways. For one, my Kur warns me of the presence of a Kjin. Secondly, he left a note for me in his office. I had just enough time to read it before the bomb went off. He tried to kill me, Kade."

He ran his hand through his hair and began pacing.

"Did you tell him about me?" she asked and then held her breath as she waited for the answer.

He snapped his head her way. "Never. I would never betray your confidence, Fallon. Tell me you believe that."

"I do," she replied and she meant it.

Suddenly, his brow creased. "You know, now that I think about it, it was him more than my parents who insisted that I stay all day yesterday."

"He probably didn't want to give you an opportunity to save me."

"Hold up. You must have realized what he was when you came to dinner at my house."

"Yes."

"And, you didn't tell me? When my family is in danger!"

"I didn't feel they were in danger at the time. Marc Ellis wants nothing more than to appear as a functional, law-abiding member of society. Your family, his family, is his cover. He would not jeopardize that."

"And, now?"

"Now, I think they may be."

He took a deep breath. "We have to find a way to keep them safe."

"We will, but that's not all." She went over to her bag and retrieved the research she printed out yesterday. She handed a copy of the newspaper article to Kade, and he scanned it carefully.

"What does the local priest have to do with any of this?"

"Father Tomas is an Emissier to Emperica. He is able to communicate with the Elders and relay information to the Knights."

Surprisingly, he did not bat an eye. "And, this murder? I was only seven or eight when it happened, but I do remember. It was big news here in Alden."

"Don't you see? Father Tomas was arrested for the murder of a child and now two children are missing."

"But, he was exonerated."

"No, the charges were dropped. How and by whom, it doesn't say in the article."

"You think he is a Kjin?"

"No, he's not. I would be able to tell if he was, but one of the Kjin that attacked us at the lake said he was summoned by the blackcoat boss. I looked it up. Blackcoat means clergyman."

"This is getting crazier and crazier. So what do we do now?"

Inside she smiled at his willingness to be in this with her. "I need to call—"

Her cell phone rang, so she stood and picked it up from the nightstand. "Hello."

"Fallon, it's me."

"Julian! I was just about to call you."

"Listen to me, Fallon! I found out that the Kjin are working together and gathering in Alden for a very specific reason."

"What is it? Why are the gathering, Julian?"

"For you, Fallon. They are gathering to kill you."

"Me? Why me?"

"Apparently, the Kjin are now organized, and the higher ups don't like the fact that you're killing so many of them. You have been named their number one target for elimination."

"How do you know all this?"

"I finally cornered that Kjin I was tracking. He spilled everything—after I let go of his throat, of course. He actually believed me when I said I'd let him go."

"You lied?" she asked.

"It was a joke, Fallon. I can't help it if the Kjin can't recognize a joke when they hear one."

She shook her head at her friend then turned to Kade who was watching her intently, obviously realizing something was wrong.

"Julian, you have to go to Buffalo."

"Buffalo?"

"Yes, you need to go to Father Michael and tell him what is going on. He probably already has a message from Darius waiting for us."

"What about Father Tomas? He is a lot closer than Father Michael."

"I have reason to believe that that particular Emissier is compromised."

Julian whistled through his teeth. "Are you sure, Fallon? That's pretty hard for me to believe."

"I know," she said regretfully. "It has been difficult for me, too."

"Okay. I'll go. But, what about you? I think it would be best if you put a little distance between yourself and Alden at this point. We'll go to Buffalo together and figure out how to handle this gathering. We may even have to call in other Knights. Nikki, for sure."

"I can't leave, Julian. Too many people will be at risk if I leave now."

His voice grew soft. "Fallon, I want to know that you'll be safe."

She glanced at Kade again—at his muscular physique and the determined look in his eye—and, a calm washed over her. "I will be safe."

"Okay. I'll call you when I get there."

"Thank you, Julian. I'll see you soon."

She hung up the phone, but before she could speak, Kade stalked over to her. "You're in danger, aren't you?"

She shrugged. "No more than usual."

He reached out and framed her face with his hands. "If...If something ever happened to you..."

"It won't," she interrupted.

With a desperate groan, he brought his face to hers and kissed her hard. She wrapped her arms around his waist and opened herself to his kiss, his passion, and his fear. Still holding her, he walked her back until her legs hit the side of the bed. His lips never left hers as they fell back and his hand began to explore her body.

"Kade..."

His body went rigid, and then he rolled off her onto his back, flinging an arm over his eyes. "I know. I'm sorry."

She sat up and looked down at him. "Don't be sorry," she murmured. "I want you as much as you want me, Kade, but I have my beliefs first and my duty second."

He peeked up at her from underneath his arm. "I've never wanted anyone more in my life than I want you, Fallon. But, not just like this. I want you in my life forever, and I want to help you in your duty to destroy the Kjin." His head dropped back down on the bed and he covered his eyes again. "I can't go back to being a cop, but helping people has always been important to me. I think we could make a pretty good team together if you'll have me."

She gently removed his arm so that he had to look at her. "I would love nothing more than to have you at my side, Kade Royce."

He looked at her doubtfully. "Really?"

She leaned down and laid her head on his chest, hugging him close. "Yes. I have my doubts, of course, but I did accept your conditions, remember?"

He stroked the side of her cheek. "You have made me a very happy man, Fallon."

"Happy to be throwing yourself into the midst of a war with evil forces? Do you really understand the danger here, Kade?"

"I do, and now that I know they exist, I couldn't walk away if I wanted to."

"I'll keep you safe," she promised him.

She felt him stiffen, but he did not respond.

"To be honest, it feels like an unending battle most of the time. The Kjin are very difficult to kill because they can easily possess another body when they have to. It would help if we had more Knights."

"I guess you will have to make do with your Knight in Shining Armor until then," he teased. "What is the plan?"

"First, removing this threat from Alden."

He growled. "My uncle, you mean."

"He's not your uncle, Kade, and the sooner you come to that realization, the easier this will be. You uncle died. How long ago, I'm not sure, but the Marc Ellis you know today is not your uncle."

He was silent for a moment. "What next, then?"

"First thing in the morning, I'm going to visit Father Tomas and get some answers."

"And, me?"

"Go to your family and suggest a vacation. Tonight. Your aunt and cousins, as well. A Kjin who has just had his human ties cut is the most dangerous of all. He will not only be looking for a new body, he will be looking for revenge."

CHAPTER 14

The Trap

What?" Marc Ellis screamed. "Are you sure of this?"

"Yes, Fallon Angell is still alive. I saw her walking toward St. Mary's before I came here."

"Was my nephew with her?"

"I didn't see him."

Marc glared at the Kjin in front of him. It was not his fault that the Knight was still alive, but Marc wanted to take his head off all the same. First, the girl managed to escape the two thugs he sent after her at the lake and now somehow escaped his bomb. "We will proceed as planned then. If that girl wishes to do this the hard way, we will do it the hard way. But, one way or another, Fallon Angell will die."

"Whatever you say," the Kjin commented dryly. His name was George Manson, a lawyer in a nearby county. He came when summoned like the good soldier he was, but Marc knew him to be ambitious. That he wanted Marc's position in the organization was assured.

Over my dead body, Manson.

Marc turned from the Kjin and glanced out of the picture window at Lake Rushden glistening in the early morning sunrise. This lake house was the perfect meeting place. His wife, Ellie, knew not to come here. He forbade her from ever stepping foot in this house without his knowledge and, after all these years, she knew better than to cross him. "How many are here?"

"Including me and you, nine. Brent Calloway is coming in from New York City tonight, but he needs another body. Cancer."

Marc waved his hand in the air. "He can have my liaison at the church."

George's eyebrows rose. "He's human?"

"Yes, but not for long," Marc sneered.

George chuckled. "Does he know that?"

"Of course not." He shrugged. "Not that it would matter much. For a human, he is quite wicked. Soulless, in fact. I don't think the transition to Kjin is going to be very hard for that one."

"What has he done?"

Marc laughed and pointed with his chin. "Have a peek inside that room on the left over there."

George looked where he indicated and made his way down the short hallway to the door.

Marc followed behind him. "Go ahead, open it."

George reached out and turned the knob, and as soon as he did, frightened squeals pierced the quiet. The door swung open and revealed two dirty, terrified children huddled in the corner.

∾

Fallon prowled around her bedroom impatiently. What was keeping Kade? After going to St. Mary's Cathedral first thing this morning and finding it empty, she immediately returned home expecting to find him here or at his house, but there was no sign of him. And, that was hours ago.

What could be keeping him?

She thought about Julian's warning again that the Kjin were gathering specifically for her. But, even more distressing was the fact that they were structured now. Just here in the northeast or all over the world? How far up the chain was Marc Ellis? Was he singularly ambitious or did even he report to someone higher?

Then, there was Father Tomas. Where did he fit in? He was not a Kjin, but why would a devoted Emissier side with evil? And, if he was that evil, why had he not changed into a Kjin yet? Suddenly, it hit her. He did not turn so he could have access to what was happening in Emperica. How much information had he already shared with his covetous rabble?

So many questions, but it was the answers that she needed to be able to protect the people of Alden.

A knock sounded on the door downstairs, and Fallon cautiously made her way down the steps. Through the side panels of the door, she saw that it was Kade and breathed a sigh of relief that he was okay. She jumped down the remaining stairs and opened the door. "What took you so long?" she asked as she threw her arms around his neck.

He lifted her off her feet and entered the house, slamming the door shut with his foot. "It was not easy to convince my family to leave town."

She untangled herself from him and could see that he was upset. "What happened?"

"I can't really blame them I guess, but they immediately jumped to the conclusion that the danger I told them they were in was from drug dealers I was associated with. They were even talking about an intervention for me."

"Drug dealers? But, your parents know you were innocent of those charges, don't they?"

"They did, but it was the first thing they thought of and, in order for them to go, I had to let them think that's what it was. What else could I tell them? That evil demons may be stopping by to steal their bodies? It was much easier for them to believe the story about drug dealers."

"I'm sorry, Kade."

"Don't be. We will get it straightened out later. Right now, their safety is the most important thing to me." He looked around the foyer nervously. "Come on, let's go up to your room. I feel like we're too exposed down here with all of the windows."

"Is that the cop talking?"

"No, the obsessed boyfriend. Now go." He pushed her ahead of him and she climbed the stairs. "What happened with Father Tomas?"

She opened the door to her bedroom and went in. "He wasn't there. Nobody was." She turned to him. "I have to get to your uncle, Kade. He tried to kill me, and he is going to be furious when he finds his family gone. He is too dangerous to leave alive."

Kade nodded. "I think I know where he may be."

She was instantly alert. "Where?"

"His lake house on Rushden."

"Why do you think he would be there?"

He raised his eyebrows. "Because I've been racking my brain about peculiar habits of his and just realized that we have never been invited there."

She was about to ask him another question, but froze when all of the lights in the house went out. She put a hand over Kade's mouth to silence him, but he shrugged her away. He was a cop, she realized. He would know not to make any noise.

She pulled her Aventi out and activated it against her arm to give them light.

The sound of glass breaking shattered the quiet. Kade gripped her arm and stepped in front of her.

Really, my dear, brave Kade?

She shook her head, but let him take the lead. He did have his conditions, after all.

Slowly, they made their way down the stairs. When they reached the bottom, Kade nodded with his head toward the kitchen and she followed behind him. As soon as Kade crossed beneath the door frame of the kitchen, he made a choking sound and slumped to the floor.

The Kur on Fallon's arm burned as she leapt over Kade's prone body and swung her Aventi at the dark figure standing over him.

Expecting only one person to be in the house, the Kjin opened his eyes wide in surprise and had no time to defend against her strike. He screamed out and fell to the ground when the Aventi penetrated his chest. The deadly black wraith burst out of the body as a roaring, angry shadow.

Kade was stirring.

She ran back to him and straddled his body, standing over him protectively with her sword of light raised in the air. "Stay down!"

Another Kjin burst through the front door. Kade ignored her warning and crawled out from beneath her shielding stance. "I'll get this one," he said, standing and running from the kitchen.

The shade in front of her tried to pursue Kade, but she held him back with the Aventi. "Not happening, Kjin. The only place you're going today is back to Mordeaux."

The demon wraith let out a frustrated, ear-splitting shriek as it zoomed around the tiny space. It only had seconds to secure a new body, and when that did not happen, it exploded apart and fell to the ground in a pile of dust.

Turning, Fallon ran out of the kitchen to help Kade, but he did not need it. She got there just in time to see his last punch knock the Kjin out cold.

"Nice," she murmured, and stabbed the evil demon with probably more force than was necessary, and this Kjin, too, burst into cinders when she thrust her Aventi at it a second time.

"Are there any more?" Kade asked, his body bladed for a fight.

She shook her head. Her Kur had gone cold. "No." She sat on the bottom step of the staircase to catch her breath. "You know, your uncle is not going to stop until I'm dead."

He sat beside her. "I would have to be dead first for that to happen," he whispered under his breath.

She reached over to touch his cheek. "Are you okay?"

"Yeah, I'm fine. The first guy karate-chopped me in the throat."

"Kade, I know you want to protect me, and I love you for that, but can I talk you into letting me do this alone?"

"No."

"This is not like anything you have ever done as a cop."

"No."

"But..."

"No."

Fallon let out a frustrated scream. "Are you always this stubborn?"

"Only where you're concerned."

"It's going to be dangerous."

"Then, why are we still sitting here talking about it?"

She took his measure for several long seconds and liked what she saw. "We leave at dark."

و

Kade turned the Jeep down a dead end street that ended at a wooden fence protecting the sandy beach of Lake Rushden. He turned off the ignition, and Fallon studied the contour of his face in the moonlight. He was so handsome. Even without a smile, his dimples were visible as he clenched his jaw in thought

"I don't like this," he muttered.

"What?"

"It feels like a trap."

"It is a trap."

He turned toward her. "Then why are we going in?"

"I'm going in because I have no choice. I have to eliminate Marc Ellis and the threat he poses to Alden. You're going in because of your *conditions*."

"About that. I decided I may have been a bit hasty with those demands."

She scrunched her face at him. "Oh, really?"

"From here on out, my only condition is the one about me helping you. I changed my mind about the bikini. You can fight in that any time."

"Kade, this is serious."

He smiled at her in the dark. "I know, Fallon. Your fellow Knight, Gabe, and I used to use humor to cover our fear all the time."

That surprised her. "Are you scared now?"

"I would be an idiot not to be. Aren't you?"

"Only for you."

He was silent for a moment. "So, Emperica really is beautiful?"

"Indescribably so. Why are you asking?"

"Because it means that no matter what happens tonight, we win. Either we are successful in eliminating my uncle or he kills us and we go to Emperica together."

She sighed and let her head fall back on the seat. "I very much look forward to returning to Emperica, Kade. More than anything. But, not until every Kjin on earth is destroyed. The people here need me, and I have sworn to protect them."

He nodded and turned back to gaze out of the windshield. "If I die tonight, I'm going to train to become a Knight and come back and find you."

Her heart clenched at the thought of him dying. "I will be a middle aged woman by then."

"It takes that long to become a Knight?"

"Thirty years. Sometimes more." She thought about Blane still in Emperica.

"That settles it then. Neither one of us is going to die tonight. I just found you and I am not going to lose you."

She ran her fingers down his cheek. "My brave, Kade."

Leaning over, he cupped her head and kissed her deeply. After several moments that left her breathless, he let go of her and opened the door. "Come on, let's get this done."

It took her a moment to pull herself together. With shaking fingers, she opened the car door and got out.

He pointed to a large cottage built on a promontory that jutted out into the lake. "That's my uncle's house. On the main drag, it's four streets over from here, but we're going to get there by the beach. Follow me."

Kade started off at a jog and she fell into step behind him. The lake was deserted at this late hour with only the moonlight and sporadic house lights to guide their way. Kade ran quickly, but she easily kept pace. As they neared the white cottage, Kade ducked behind a sandy berm that concealed their passage the rest of the way. Just under the outcrop where the house was built, Kade put his hand up and they stopped.

Fallon looked up. The cottage was completely dark. All of the coiled up adrenaline in her body fled from her in a frustrated exhaled breath. She thought for sure, he would be here, and she just wanted to end this. Now.

Kade turned to her. "It doesn't look like anyone is here. Should we come back?"

She thought about it for a moment. Should they try and track Marc Ellis at his residence? Or, try to find Father Tomas again? "Let's go in," she finally decided. "Maybe he left behind some clues."

"As long as it isn't a bomb," Kade muttered, and together they ran up the wooden stairs that led from the beach to the wide covered porch of the house. Silently, Kade walked across the deck and tried the door. It was unlocked.

Kade gave her a suspicious glance and went inside at a crouch, keeping his silhouette as small as possible. Fallon followed suit, wishing she had more light, but not daring to light the Aventi that would just put a target on their backs if anybody was in the house.

The place was completely silent.

"You go upstairs," she suggested. "I'll look down here."

While Kade climbed to the second level, Fallon searched through the rooms. It was a very luxurious home with the best of everything, but she did notice that it did not have the touch of a woman here. There were no prints or flowers or toys or family photos. This was a place for Marc Ellis alone and not his family.

What are you hiding here, Mr. Ellis?

Fallon made her way down a hallway off the kitchen. There were two doors off the corridor and both were closed. She walked to the one on the right first and opened the door a few inches. Reaching inside, she felt along the wall and flicked on the light.

It was a laundry room. And, empty.

Closing the door, she went to the room on the left.

She opened this door cautiously as well, and found the switch easily, sending light flooding through the room. It was a small bedroom, and it, too, was empty.

She started to close the door, but stopped when she heard a very faint rustling noise.

Somebody was in there.

Marc Ellis? Another Kjin? No, her Kur had not given warning.

She opened the door wide and stepped inside, pulling her Aventi from her back pocket. There was no closet where a man could be hiding, so she dropped to the ground to look under the bed.

No one was there.

Standing, she noticed a wide wardrobe in the corner and made her way toward it. She heard the noise again. There was something in the wardrobe. Shrugging her left arm out of her hoodie, she lifted the Aventi and made contact with the Kur, igniting the weapon.

Without hesitation, she threw open the cabinet doors.

"Oh, crap," she murmured at the sight of two children with duck tape over their mouths and wrists.

A boy and a girl. The two missing children.

She leaned down toward them, and they shrank back from her in fright.

"It's okay," she reassured them. "I'm here to help. I promise."

She reached out and peeled the tape from the boy first and then the girl.

"Are you hurt?" she asked them.

Both children shook their heads.

"I just want my Mommy," the girl cried.

Fallon pulled the little girl from the wardrobe and held her tight. "I will take you to your Mommy. Can you walk?"

She nodded, so Fallon put her down and helped the boy out.

"Is the mean man gone?" the boy asked.

"I think so, but we better get out of here. I have a friend upstairs and he will help us."

Fallon ushered the children toward the door. "Quickly now, go into the kitchen."

The children ran out of the room and, too late, Fallon felt the burn on her arm. Just as she stepped out of the room, an arm snaked out of the hallway and covered her mouth.

"Listen up! I know you can kill me, but if you want those children and your little boyfriend to survive the night, send them away. Now!"

Fallon elbowed the Kjin in the face and broke his nose. Spinning, she grabbed him under the throat and slammed him against the wall.

"Last warning, Knight! The place is surrounded. If you kill me now, your boyfriend and the children will die!"

CHAPTER 15

An Unlikely Hero

Fallon's arms trembled in anger as she reconciled herself to the fact that she had little choice in the matter. She let the Kjin fall to the floor. "You better hide, then. If my *little* boyfriend sees you, I will never be able to convince him to leave."

The Kjin scrambled to his feet. "And, tell him not to bring up Marc Ellis' name to the police," he warned her before disappearing into the bedroom.

She took a deep breath and walked into the kitchen. The children were huddled together, but broke apart and ran to her when they saw Kade coming down the stairs with a look of utter disbelief on his face.

Fallon bent down to them and began to remove the duck tape around their wrists. "Don't be afraid. This is my friend, Kade, and he is going to take you to the police station, okay?"

"No! We want you to take us!"

She shook her head. "I can't, but I promise that Kade is a very good guy, and he is going to take you to your parents. Okay?"

Reluctantly, they nodded.

"You're coming, too," Kade said, his tone determined.

"Kade, just take them for me, please. I still have to track your uncle."

"We'll drop them off together and then go to my uncle's house. I can show you where he lives."

"Just give me the address. There's no need for both of us to go to the police station."

He narrowed his eyes at her.

"Please, Kade. They are so defenseless. They have been through too much already. Just take them to the police, and I will call you and let you know where I am."

"Did you find some kind of lead?" he asked, suspiciously.

She nodded. She did find a lead. It was a big, evil Kjin, and she had no doubt that he would lead her directly to Professor Marc Ellis.

Kade grasped her shoulders hard enough to make her wince. He knew something was not quite right. "I don't want to leave you."

"I know, but you have to."

He looked over at the children and then back at her as if searching for an argument. In the end, he could not find one. "Call me within fifteen minutes and let me know exactly where you are. I'll meet you." He went into the kitchen and found a pad of paper and pen.

After scribbling the address down, he handed it to her. "Be careful."

"I will. I love you."

"I love you, too. More than anything."

She swallowed past the pain in her throat when she realized that this was the last time she would ever see Kade Royce. Impulsively, she flung her arms around his neck and held him close, inhaling the scent of him. She could only describe his smell as masculine spice. So unique. So Kade.

Finally, she broke away, and Kade faced the children. "Okay, guys, ready to go home?"

The two children squealed and ran to him. He took one tiny hand in each of his and led them to the door with the big porch. "Fifteen minutes," he reminded before picking up the kids and running off toward the beach.

"Goodbye, Kade," she had time to whisper before a needle pierced her arm and darkness swallowed her.

❧

Twenty minutes after leaving Fallon, Kade walked into the Alden Police Department and into complete chaos. He had already called ahead, so the parents were waiting along with a reporter and single cameraman. He knew it would not be long before more showed up. The story of the missing children had been nationwide news for over a month now.

Fallon hasn't called yet. Why?

"Mommy! Daddy!"

Kade let go of the kids, and they ran into the waiting arms of their parents.

The Chief of Police immediately came up to him and gave him a terse nod. "Royce."

"Chief."

"Can we get a statement, Chief Mignore?" interrupted the young, local reporter, a woman with short blonde hair.

The Chief scowled. "Not yet. I'll have something for you in a few minutes."

Where are you, Fallon?

Kade started for the door.

"Royce! You're not going anywhere, my friend. I have a lot of questions for you."

Kade ran his hand through his hair. This was going to take more time than he was willing to give. He had to think of something fast.

"Where?"

"Interrogation Three. Now."

Reluctantly, he followed his former boss into the small room.

"Start at the beginning," Chief Mignore said, plopping down into one of the two chairs in the room. "Wait." He got up again. "Gates! Stevie Gates! Bring two coffees in here." Shutting the door, he sat back down.

Kade thought about his story on the way and decided it was best to make it as simple as possible. "I found the kids at my uncle's lake house."

"Your uncle? Marc Ellis?"

"Yeah."

"And, why would two missing children be at your uncle's lake house?"

"I don't know."

The Chief slammed his fist down. "Stop playing games with me, Royce! Tell me what happened and don't force me to drag it out of you one morsel at a time!"

"I honestly don't know! Your questions should be directed at my uncle, not me!"

The door opened and Deputy Gates set two cups on the table and, after seeing the looks on both of their faces, quickly left.

Chief Mignore rubbed his chin. "Did you ask him?"

"He wasn't at the house. I went there to talk to my uncle and when I went in, I found the kids. I don't know how they got there or who left them." He leaned forward across the table. "You know me, Chief. That is the truth of it. I swear."

"There has to be more."

"There is no more! I went to my uncle's house, and I found the kids there. Trust me, I am going to find my uncle and get to the bottom of this."

"You're not an officer anymore, Royce," the Chief reminded brutally.

"Look, if you're going to arrest me on some trumped up charge, do it! I've been there before! If not, I'd like to leave."

The Chief leaned back in his chair and entwined his fingers over his ample stomach. "So, you are just the hero in all of this? Is that what you want me to believe?"

"I am no hero. I stumbled across the kids and did what any other law-abiding citizen would do."

The Chief lifted his eyebrow at the law-abiding reference.

"Are you going to arrest me?" he demanded again.

The Chief took a sip of his coffee and stared at him over the top of the cup. "I haven't decided yet."

Kade threw his hands in the air and cursed.

"But," the Chief interjected, "do I think you kidnapped these children? No. I don't. But, I don't think you have told me everything you know either."

Kade stood and put both hands on the table. "Let me out of here, and I will get you your answers. I promise."

The Chief was silent for several moments. "First, I want you to go out there and smile for the press and let Alden have their hero story. Then, you can go and get me my answers."

"Great Tyras, but you are a very hard person to kill, Miss Angell."

Fallon groaned and opened one eye. The figure sitting in a chair across from her was blurry, but she knew without a doubt that it was Marc Ellis. Clean shaven, square glasses, and the sweater vests he seemed to enjoy.

She tried to wipe her eyes, but the movement caused shooting pain to radiate up her arms. She realized then that her wrists were chained above her head. Sitting on a cold cement floor with her legs curled to the side, she tugged at her shackles, but the effort only brought more agony to her raw skin.

"Where am I?" she asked, groggily.

"Oh, not to worry about that, my dear. No one will interrupt us if that is what you're concerned about. I can assure you of that."

"Tell me, Kjin. How long have you been masquerading as Marc Ellis?"

The Kjin got up from the chair in front of her and walked over to a cheap, aluminum desk near the wall. She could now see that they were in a cavernous office space that looked like it belonged in an industrial warehouse.

"Too many years to count, young Knight." Fallon heard laughter coming from beyond the only door to the room. "Must be another soldier has joined us," Marc mused aloud.

Soldier? What was he talking about? "What do you want with me?" she asked, already knowing the answer.

"To kill you, of course."

Fallon swallowed and said. "So, why haven't you done it already? You had plenty of time after you drugged me."

"Tsk, tsk. In such a hurry to return to Emperica? Well, you must wait a little while longer. Our numbers are short at the moment, and we are still waiting for another guest to make his appearance."

A Ha'Basin.

Fallon struggled with her chains again, but she was weak from the drugs she had been given and they did not budge.

Marc crossed over to a television set mounted in the corner of the room. "Until then, let's see just how bad the Alden Police are mangling this investigation. They wouldn't be able to figure this out if I painted a picture for them."

The voice of a news anchor boomed across the room. "Sarah, what more can you tell us about this developing story?" The screen cut to a shot of a young, blonde reporter standing in front of the Alden Police Department. "Thank you, Jane. At this hour, I can confirm that the children are unharmed and reunited with their parents. Earlier, we reported that former police officer, Kade Royce, was the person who actually rescued the children, and I have that hero with us now. Kade, can I ask you a few questions?"

The camera zoomed out and panned to the right.

Fallon's breath caught when she saw Kade's face on the screen. *Good. He is safe.*

"How does it feel to know you were the one responsible for saving the lives of two children?" she asked and shoved a black microphone under his mouth.

"I...I'm just glad they are home."

"You are a hero, Kade Royce."

"No, I'm not."

She laughed. "Well, I think we have thousands of viewers, myself included, that would disagree with you on that one."

"Look, I am grateful the kids are home, I really am. But, there is something I have to take care of right now. If you will excuse me."

The reporter looked confused. "A few more questions..."

Kade shook his head. "Sorry, I really have to go. But, here is Chief Mignore," Kade said as he waved the camera over to the Chief of Police. "He would love to answer any other questions you have."

Fallon noticed the Chief's frown a fraction of a second before he plastered on a polite smile for the camera. "Is it true, Chief Mignore, that the children were found in the home of the President of Alden University, Marc Ellis?"

"What?" thundered Marc. "He gave them my name?"

"Yes, it is—"

The television went silent when Marc Ellis pulled it from the wall and it crashed to the concrete floor.

"Does he care nothing for you?" Marc screamed at her. "He would jeopardize your life?"

"Oh, that's my fault. It actually slipped my mind to give him your message."

The Kjin's face turned dangerously red. "You think you're funny? I should have killed you, him and the kids when I had the chance."

"So, why didn't you?" she shouted and then regretted it when her head exploded in pain.

"You had your Aventi! We never could have killed you or drugged you unless you allowed it. And, that could only happen if we threatened your precious Kade and the children."

"You're disgusting."

He smiled. "Now, though, I'm glad I didn't kill Kade. Obviously, I can't go around as Marc Ellis any longer thanks to him, so I'll just take his body in recompense. Oh, yes, just think of what I can accomplish here in Alden as the local hero."

Fallon screamed out at him and got to her feet. "Leave him alone, you monster!"

"Did I touch a nerve, Knight? Do you love my little nephew? Will you love me just as much when I have his body?"

"I will kill you, Kjin!"

He gestured to her chains. "That is going to be a little hard to do, my dear." He walked closer to her. "Let me finish my story. We needed to let Kade and the children go to drug you, true. But, the reason we haven't killed you yet? It is because Tyras wants to send a message to your Creator with a little Ha'Basin. When you return, we want you to tell him that his precious earth is no longer the Eden he hoped for, and it hasn't been for a very long time. We are organized now and we are winning, Knight! And, who is doing most of our work for us? The humans!"

"No."

"Yes! We are converting more and more to our side every day. We can't make them all Kjin, but we don't have to. Humans are greedy and arrogant little creatures. Believe me, with the right incentives, it hasn't been very difficult to turn many of them to our cause."

"No."

"Deny it if you will, Knight. In the age old battle of good versus evil, the tide is finally turning in our favor."

"I will not believe your lies, Kjin, because I am not weak in my faith. Humans are inherently good and selfless, and I have seen proof of that fact time and time again."

Marc waved a hand in the air. "Deceive yourself all you want. When you return to Emperica, you will see the truth easily enough."

Fallon lifted her hands with a shriek to pull on the chain above her again, but her strength was too diminished. She just did not have the power to free herself. Marc Ellis knew this and laughed at her when her futile efforts only caused her to cry out from the pain. Not the physical pain. The pain of knowing that she had failed. Darius entrusted her with saving the mortals in her care, and she failed after only four years.

What about Kade? Her brave Kade. She knew she would never see him again, but what if Marc Ellis held true to his word and took possession of his body? Thinking of Kade trapped in that nightmare for the rest of his life broke her.

She slumped back to the ground and, although she tried to hold back her tears, she could not do it. Worse, because of the chains, she couldn't wipe them away. Not for one second did she want to give this evil demon the satisfaction of thinking she was defeated.

"A Knight of Emperica crying?" Marc Ellis taunted through her agonized thoughts.

"I don't cry because of you, Kjin! I cry because I love. Because I feel. You won't make me feel ashamed for doing so."

"Weak," he muttered.

She was angry now. "No! Not weak. The bonds of love are far stronger than the hatred you spew. I promise that you will be destroyed very soon, Kjin! If not by me, then by the next Knight who comes looking for you."

The door banged open, and now Fallon had another target for her anger. Her blood boiled at the sight of the confidante that betrayed her and Emperica so absolutely.

She glared at Father Tomas as he stood in the entrance to the room and smiled at her.

CHAPTER 16

The Traitor

Marc Ellis turned to follow her gaze and waved the priest in. "Come on in, Father, and join the party."

Father Tomas walked in hesitantly and then fell to the floor on his hands and knees with a grunt.

Fallon gasped.

Standing behind the priest with an evil smile spread across his face was Father Tomas' altar boy, Anthony.

"Father, please go sit by your Knight," Marc gestured. "Come, Anthony, we have much to discuss."

Anthony gave Father Tomas a prodding kick and then followed Marc out of the room.

"Father! Are you all right?" Fallon cried.

The old man nodded and staggered to his feet. His lip was bleeding and he had a fresh gash on his right cheek. "Yes, I am fine." He walked over to her on shaky legs and sat down beside her. Looking up at her shackles with a frown, she saw tears form in his eyes. "I wish I could free you, Fallon. Are you in much pain?"

The muscles in her arms and shoulders ached in a constant throb, but she merely shook her head at him. "I can manage. Tell me what is going on here? I thought you were working with Marc Ellis?"

He gave her a bewildering look. "Me? My goodness, child, you really thought that?"

Embarrassed, Fallon nodded. "I...I saw a newspaper article about your arrest for murdering a child fifteen years ago." She shook her head. "You didn't do it, did you? What a fool I was to believe that obvious plant from Anthony."

"I did do it."

She snapped her head toward him. "You did?"

"Yes. I did kill that child and it was the hardest thing I ever had to do in my life. But, she was not a human child, Fallon. She was a Kjin. As soon as I figured out what she was, I plotted to kill her. I should have summoned a Knight to do it, but I didn't. Unfortunately, I was caught in the act by my altar boy at the time and he turned me into the authorities. It was his word against mine, and in the end, Bishop Tierney helped me to beat the charge by discrediting the boy."

"I...I'm sorry, Father. I should never have believed you could be capable of such a crime." She paused. "But, wait. The Kjin said they were summoned by the head blackcoat. Blackcoat means clergyman."

"If you had looked at the secondary definition, you would have read that it also means soldier. That is what the newly ordered Kjin are calling themselves. Soldiers. They have declared war against Emperica."

"And, Anthony is working with them?"

"I am afraid so. Is he one of them yet?" he asked her.

Fallon shook her head. "No. He is still human."

"Maybe there is hope for the boy yet," the priest murmured. He was silent for a few moments, but his face grew more tortured. "There is no way out for either of us, Fallon. They will kill me outright and perform the Ha'Basin for you."

"I suspected as much. We should make peace with our deaths here on earth, Father." She gave him a resigned smile. "It is my solemn hope that we meet again in Emperica. Shall we pray?" The words came out calmly, but felt like broken glass in her mouth as she spoke them. *Goodbye, Kade. I hope you can evade your uncle and find peace in this world. Until we meet again, my love.*

Father Tomas interrupted her thoughts. "Fallon, unless you agree to help me, I won't be going to Emperica."

She glanced at him. "What do you mean?"

"I overheard one of the Kjin talking. The body he has is full of cancer, and he needs a new body right away. I may be old, but I fear he is going to take mine. If he does, my soul will be locked away while the Kjin uses me for evil purpose. I could not bear that, Fallon."

Her heart skipped a beat when she understood what he intended for her to do. "How would you have me help you?"

"Kill me."

"Father..."

"I am so tired, Fallon. I just want to go home. Please release me."

She shook her head violently. "You know I can't do that! Please don't ask that of me."

His eyes were reddened from his tears. "I have dedicated a lifetime of service to the Creator. I wish to be pure when I meet him for the first time. I cannot allow a Kjin to inhabit my body. Ever! Please, Fallon," he begged, "do this for me. I know how difficult this request is for you, but I will not go to my Creator tainted by evil! I will not!"

"Father! I...I have no weapon to use." Was she really considering this?

"You can use your legs. You can wrap them around—"

"I can't!" she screamed at him in horror.

Panicked by her refusal, the priest glanced wildly around the large room. Spotting the broken television set on the ground, he scrambled to his feet and rushed to the broken glass. He pried a piece loose and came back to kneel in front of her.

She turned away from him. "I can't wield that glass with my legs, Father."

"I know, but I can," he whispered. "Do you think the Creator will forgive me, Fallon?"

She turned back and her heart broke for him. "I do."

"Pray with me?"

"Yes, of course."

He put his hand on her leg, bowed his head, and prayed to the heavenly Creator for forgiveness for what he was about to do. When he was finished, goose bumps rose on her arms at the last desperate look he gave her. "I'm sorry to be leaving you alone, Fallon, but I can think of no other way."

"Do what you think is right, Father. I will not judge you."

He nodded once more, and she swallowed back her scream as Father Tomas plunged the broken glass into the artery on his neck. Blood gushed from the wound as he sank down beside her.

It took several agonizing moments for him to die. Unable to touch him or comfort him, Fallon continued to murmur words of prayer over his body until he drew his last breath.

Almost immediately, the familiar black tunnel appeared in the room and a white light twinkled in the distance. This time, however, the light approached them through the tunnel, growing larger as it drew near.

Fallon sobbed tears of joy as Father Tomas' spirit lifted from the corpse on the ground and he was free at last. The wide smile on the priest's face, in such contrast to the torment of moments before spoke to the true miracle of death. Father Tomas beamed as he looked around the room in wonder that he had crossed over.

A white-robed Sentinel appeared at the entrance of the tunnel, and Fallon noted with a smile that it was Josiah. Father Tomas was getting his own personal escort to Emperica and, as far as she was concerned, there was no one better for the task.

"Over here, Father! Quickly now!" Josiah shouted with the same enthusiasm Fallon remembered. "There are many people coming home today!"

The Sentinel looked over at her with a cringe. "Oh, dear. I am so sorry, Knight, that I cannot help you. The affairs of earth are not something I can get involved in."

"I know. It's okay, Josiah."

Josiah's face softened. "Fallon?"

"Yes. I am honored that you remembered," she said with a slight bow of her head.

The Sentinel smiled. "Of course I remember. I cannot do anything for you now, but I promise you this. I will be waiting for you when you return home."

"I will be looking forward to it."

Fallon watched Father Tomas glide toward the waiting guide. After a lifetime of devotional service, the euphoria on his face was contagious, and even the Sentinel could not help but laugh out loud.

"Yes, it is a wonderful day for you, Father. I have been doing this for so long that sometimes I forget the pure ecstasy of the moment." He gestured. "Come now. We will talk along the way. A special welcome is in store for you."

Father Tomas burst into tears, but looked back at Fallon one more time and whispered, "I'm sorry." Then, he was gone. The tunnel disappeared behind him and she was alone.

Fallon hung her head in fearful exhaustion. Although overjoyed for Father Tomas, she realized that she did not want to die tonight.

She had always known that she would die again in service of the Knights, but now, because of Kade Royce, she only hoped that it would not be tonight.

CHAPTER 17

The Pawn

Fallon did not die last night. The Kjin never returned that evening and she was left alone, hanging by her shackles with Father Tomas' body next to her. Every once in awhile, she would fall into fitful sleep, but she would soon awaken from the pain and the nightmares. It had to be morning now although there were no windows to confirm her suspicion.

She looked up when the door banged open and Anthony barged in.

The young altar boy seemed so innocent to Fallon all those times she met him at the church, but with the pretense of goodness stripped away and his features screwed up in malice, he looked anything but.

The focus of his hatred was not her, though. It was the body lying at her feet.

"What a filthy coward!"

She really did not want to speak to the boy, but refused to let this harborer of evil desecrate the Emissier's memory. "Coward? Father Tomas was one of the bravest men I ever knew!"

"Taking your own life is brave?" he scoffed.

"Yes, when the alternative is to live as a Kjin."

"Kjin? What are you talking about?"

So, he did not yet know that he was dealing with the supernatural. This kid had no idea what he had gotten himself into. What then was his motive?

"Why do you hate Father Tomas so much, Anthony?"

The boy glared at her as if the answer should have been obvious. "Why? Because he's a child killer, that's why. You saw the article I *dropped* at your feet, didn't you?"

Fallon knew there had to be more. Something personal. "And, you just took it upon yourself to seek justice for this child? After fifteen years?"

He strode directly to where she was tethered and stared down at her with a sneer. "Don't be stupid. I hate the priest for what he did to my brother."

"Your brother?"

"Yeah, he witnessed with his own eyes Father Tomas murder that little girl, Lilly, and he was never the same again after that with all of the members of the church ganging up on him and calling him a liar. My parents had to send him away to a mental institution." He kicked Father Tomas' body. "This murderer killed two kids that day. A girl and a boy."

A girl and a boy. Suddenly, it dawned on her. "The kidnapped kids? It wasn't Marc Ellis, it was you."

"Of course it was me! Haven't you been listening to me? I had it all planned out to kidnap the kids and frame Father Tomas for it. I wasn't going to let this jerk get away with what he did! As soon as he saw the lilies I left at the rectory, he should have known his days were numbered." He stared at the body on the floor with venom in his eyes. "But, it looks like the coward got away with it anyway. He deserved to suffer for what he did."

Fallon could not believe that Father Tomas never saw how depraved this young man was. But, he fooled her, too.

"Where is Marc now?" she asked him, wondering just how much time she had left.

"Getting ready."

"For what?"

"Are you that thick? Really?"

Anthony began moving the few furniture items in the room against the walls, leaving the center clear.

"How did you get involved with Marc Ellis?" If she was going to return to Emperica today, at least she would bring back as much information to Darius as she could. While the Elders were able to see some things in this world, they were not omnipresent. They could not see everything. And, this fight would continue long after Fallon returned home.

He shrugged. "Somehow he found out I had a grudge with the priest and offered to help me with my plans to kidnap the kids and hide them." He shrugged. "He said he was trying to lure someone here, and the crimes had to be pretty major. He also said Father Tomas was *on to him*. Whatever that meant."

"What did he promise you?" Fallon asked, remembering Marc Ellis' comment that it was easy to sway humans to his side.

"Money."

"That's all?"

"What else is there?"

"You would give up your soul for a little bit of cash?"

"Giving up my soul? What are you, some kind of religious fanatic? It's a no-brainer. Marc is going to pay me some serious cash to do things for him. Easy stuff at first, like bringing Father Tomas here, but later he said I'll get to do more."

"Your soul is worth more than that."

"Why did you keep talking about my soul? Jeez."

"Because any minute now, one of Marc's friends is going to come in here and take it from you. He is going to come in and forcefully take possession of your body by unleashing a demon spirit into you. After the possession is complete, your soul will be locked away in tormented witness to all the acts you will commit beyond your control."

Anthony backed away from her with his hands in the air. "Whoa! Those drugs must have really messed you up."

"No, it's the truth."

"Even if what you're talking about wasn't a made-up fairytale, Marc wouldn't betray me to anybody."

"Marc Ellis is a demon, Anthony. Tell me. How many of his friends have gathered here?"

"I think there's ten of them."

"And, one is sick with disease. He will seek out your body and for years and years, you will be nothing but a mute passenger to the rest of your life. Then, when, your body finally dies, your soul will be sent to the fiery hell of Mordeaux."

"Don't be ridiculous..."

"You had eternal life in heaven!" she exploded. "And, you threw it all way for some cash. The sad thing is, you aren't even going to get a chance to spend it. You're going to die here today, just like I am."

"I don't believe you! Plus, why should I care about trying to get into heaven. Everybody knows it doesn't really exist. It's just a made up place to get everybody to stay in line."

"It does exist, Anthony. I promise you that."

"I knew it! You are a fanatic!"

"No. I'm an angel."

"Oh, I've heard it all now! Angels and demons?" His threw his head back and laughed, but it was cut off abruptly when the door opened and Marc Ellis walked in with another man a bit older and with a sickly, yellow pallor.

"Marc! I'm glad you're here. You wouldn't believe the stuff this girl is saying."

"What would that be, Anthony?"

"She actually wants me to believe that she is an angel and you're a demon. And, get this. You're going to try and *steal* my soul." He walked over to Marc and patted him on the shoulder with a grin.

Marc appeared to be thinking about it and then nodded. "That pretty much sums it up."

The grin faded from the boy's face. "Cut it out, Marc. This is not funny."

"Humor is the farthest thing from my mind at the moment, Anthony."

"So, you want me to believe that you were just using me to bring Father Tomas here and now you're going to give my...my body to one of your friends? Come on! What's going on here?"

"I was actually going to take your body for myself, but Brent here needs it more than I do. Besides, I have another picked out for me." He looked skyward. "I always did love a hero's welcome."

Fallon screamed at him in fury.

Anthony backed away in horror. "No! Get away from me!"

Fallon closed her eyes, not wanting to witness what was about to happen. But, when Anthony sprinted to her and collapsed beside her on the floor, she opened them again.

"Save me!"

"I wish I could," she whispered. She knew it was useless but tried anyway. "Marc, let him go. He's just a boy."

Marc ignored her plea as Brent advanced toward them. When Anthony realized she could provide no assistance, he got up and ran. More agile than she thought possible, the old man tackled Anthony around the waist and brought him to the floor.

"No!" The bloodcurdling cry felt like a physical blow to Fallon's heart.

"Marc, hold him for me!" Brent demanded.

Marc Ellis walked over to the struggling duo and lifted Anthony from the ground and held him still by his elbows.

"Stop! Please! I want to live." The last words were a murmured whimper.

Brent put both of his hands on either side of Anthony's face, hovered his mouth over the boy's mouth and inhaled deeply. A human would not be able to see what was happening, but Fallon saw every grotesque detail.

At first, nothing happened, but then a stream of white mist flowed from Anthony's mouth into Brent's. The boy's eyes bulged, but the rest of his body went rigid, paralyzed now in the sorcerous grip of an ancient dark magic that once started, could not be broken.

As Anthony's soul surged out of his body, Fallon thought of this happening to Kade and she turned to the side and retched.

"I have it," Brent said hoarsely and Fallon could not help herself. She looked back up.

With a violent cough, Brent breathed the now black vapor back into Anthony's body. The sinister torrent seemed to flood endlessly into the young boy, and when the last sinuous tendril finally disappeared into his mouth, both bodies collapsed to the ground.

A moment later, the body of Anthony stood, but not a trace of the boy remained.

"Much better," Brent said through Anthony's mouth.

"Oh, to be sixteen again," Marc laughed.

Fallon felt sick again. "I have had enough of your disgusting evil," she told him. "Get your ten in here and get on with this. I don't want to be in your presence another second longer!"

"My thoughts exactly. But, you will have to wait until this evening. For what we have planned for you, darkness is best."

CHAPTER 18

The Devil

One by one, the Kjin blackcoats entered the room, and Fallon watched them come with resigned acceptance. They looked remarkably normal. Fathers, grandfathers, young men, and even a soldier in his military uniform.

With ordered efficiency, they removed the two bodies lying on the floor and formed a circle in the center of the room.

Fallon bowed her head to pray and almost instantly, she felt a sense of peace flow through her mind and body. When at last she lifted her eyes to her ten executioners, she found that she was no longer afraid. The ache in her arms, the hunger and thirst, and even the weariness seemed lessened.

Marc Ellis approached and stood before her. "Fallon Angell, Knight of Emperica, the all mighty Tyras, King of Mordeaux, has declared you an enemy of the Kjin. In his wisdom, he has ordered the Ha'Basin to expel you from this world to snivel at the feet of your master for all time."

She smiled. "Can't wait."

He pulled his glasses from his face and began to clean them with the hem of his shirt. "I don't think you would be so excited, my dear, if you knew the truth."

"What would you know about truth, Kjin?"

"I know the truth of this because I experienced it firsthand when I came to earth. Let me just say that the Ha'Basin is not pleasant."

"No?" she asked with feigned disinterest.

He leaned down close to her and she could feel his breath on her face. "As soon as you pass through the eye of the magic, the first thing you will feel is a scorching burn. It will progressively grow worse until your skin begins to bubble like molten lava. After that, all of the bones in your body will feel like they are breaking. One by one. And, finally, just before you meet your Creator for the second time, your brain will explode with the pain of a hundred needles plunging into your temples." He straightened and put his glasses back on his face. "Of course, the pain will fall away as soon as you enter Emperica, but until that time, you will wish I had sent you to Mordeaux instead."

Fallon gave him an icy glare. "Never."

Marc simply shrugged. "I'll never know in any case. Goodbye, my dear." He turned back to the other Kjin in the room. "Let us begin the ritual." Taking his place in the circle, he lifted his arms and his voice filled the room. "Mighty Tyras! Your faithful have come together to carry out the Ha'Basin. With this power you grant to us, we will cast your adversary, the Knight, Fallon Angell, back to Emperica!"

Fallon could only look on helplessly as in unison the other Kjin joined Marc Ellis in their dark chant. *"With souls forged from the fires beyond, darkness and chaos seal our bond. Oh, King Tyras, show us your might, sever the life of this enemy Knight."*

All of a sudden, Marc Ellis cut off the chant and his hands flew to his throat as a gurgling sound erupted from his mouth. His eyes widened in terror as his body began convulsing in spasms so violent that Fallon was surprised he could remain on his feet. Several of the other Kjin cried out and shrank back from their trembling leader. It seemed she was not the only one shocked by what was happening.

Marc Ellis' eyes rolled up into his head until only the whites were showing, and then he stopped moving and the room went silent.

Fallon felt a cold shiver run up her spine.

After another powerful shudder raked his entire body, Marc's mouth opened abnormally wide, and a guttural, sinister laugh echoed throughout the room.

Fallon cringed. The countenance on Marc Ellis' face was evil personified.

It was the devil.

"My faithful," purred the voice that now emanated from Marc, and the rest of the Kjin immediately dropped to their knees in submission.

Fallon heard their scared whispers.

"Tyras!"

"How can that be? It's Tyras!"

The voice spoke again, silencing the room. "You have done well, my faithful, and you will be rewarded for your efforts when you join me in Mordeaux. Until then, we have much work to do." The white eyes turned toward Fallon and it took every bit of strength she possessed not to cower from him.

He began walking to her haltingly with stilted, unnatural steps. It seemed the devil had control not only of Marc Ellis' mind, but his body as well. Fallon wondered how it was possible that he was able to exert that much power here on earth. His seal should have prevented this from happening.

"Fallon Angell." The sibilant sound of her name on the tongue of the devil enraged her, but she found that she could not turn her head away from him. Somehow, he was holding her fast in his invisible, wicked grasp. "My words to you will be brief by necessity. While the seal to Mordeaux is weakening, it confines me still. You are here today at this Ha'Basin so you can relay a message back to your Creator."

She wanted to scream at him, kick out at his white-eyed gaze, but she could do neither, paralyzed by the curse of his presence.

"You will tell him that Tyras has declared war on Emperica! For thousands of years, the Knights of Emperica have hunted the Kjin, but from this day forward, the Kjin will hunt the Knights! Our powers are growing. A portal is opening. Earth will soon be mine, Fallon Angell! Tell your Creator that earth is mine!"

Marc Ellis' body fell to the ground in a heap, and Fallon let out a gasp as the unseen bond that held her disappeared and she could breathe normally again.

The Anthony Kjin walked over and helped his disoriented leader back to his feet. "I didn't know that Tyras could enter this world," he commented with a slight tremor in his voice.

Marc opened his eyes and although they were his normal color again, he looked quite shaken by the invasion of his body. "I didn't think he could either."

Fallon strained against her bonds. She had to do something! She could not leave now with Emperica and Mordeaux poised on the brink of war! If fighting broke out between these two powerful forces, all of humankind would be lost in the struggle.

Marc ignored her. "Let's continue." He walked back to the circle, but the Anthony Kjin held back.

"Aren't you going to remove her restraints?" he asked.

Marc shook his head. "Not until we are at full power." He looked at each Kjin in his circle. "Let us continue the Ha'Basin. The chant must be delivered three times to be at full power."

"*With souls forged from the fires beyond, darkness and chaos seal our bond. Oh, King Tyras, show us your might, sever the life of this enemy Knight.*"

This is it, she thought. I now leave earth for the last time. Tears began to trace a slow path down her face.

Oh, Kade! Would she forget about him once she was back in Emperica? Could she?

"With souls forged from the fires beyond, darkness and chaos seal our bond. Oh, King Tyras, show us your might, sever the life of this enemy Knight."

A sudden breeze began to swirl around the large room. As the chanting grew louder and more fervent, so did the wind. She had to squint her eyes as her long hair whipped around her head.

They were opening the gateway.

"With souls forged from the fires beyond, darkness and chaos seal our bond. Oh, King Tyras, show us your might, sever the life of this enemy Knight."

In the center of the spinning mass, a funneled shaft appeared. From the floor, she felt the strengthening pull of the vortex. Her body slid on the ground toward the swirling eddy, but the chain holding her wrists stopped her momentum. She screamed out at the pain, the metal biting cruelly into her already tender skin.

She jumped to her feet to try to relieve some of the pressure on her wrists, but her legs were swept out from under her in the growing storm. She floated above the floor now, secured only by her iron tether.

"We are at full power!" Marc Ellis shouted. "Keep up the chant and at the cost of your lives, do not stop!"

Marc slipped from the group, still murmuring words under his breath.

As he neared, she kicked her leg toward his face. She smiled at the small victory as her foot connected with his jaw and he cursed at her.

She looked back to the center of the room. The gateway was fully open now, and a glowing white light appeared in the middle of the whirlpool. As soon as Marc unlocked her shackles, she would be powerless to fight the strength of the currents and her body would be sucked through. Then, the pain would begin.

Marc was also having trouble staying on his feet, and he grabbed her chain to anchor himself.

She tried to kick out at him again, but he was now out of reach of her attacks.

"It has been nice knowing you, Knight," he hissed in her ear and lifted a small key to the lock on her wrists.

Over the tumultuous noise of the wind, Fallon heard the door to the room slam open.

Several of the Kjin stopped their chant to look, but Marc Ellis screamed at them. "Don't stop! Do not stop!"

"A party! I love parties," said a boisterous voice from the doorway.

Fallon wanted to cry when she heard the familiar voice. Not the tears of joy for a rescue, but the tears of terror. Her savior did not stand a chance of surviving.

CHAPTER 19

Friendship Lost

Oh, Julian, no! Get out of here while you still can!
What was he doing here? He was supposed to be on his
way to Buffalo.

The wind started to lesson from the interruption.

"Keep chanting! I'll take care of this!" yelled Marc and
ran to confront Julian.

"Julian! It is a Ha'Basin! Get out!" she screamed over
the Kjin voices, lost once more in their evil mantra.

"Full power! I need full power!" ordered Marc.

In response to the demand, the chant grew louder and
the wind stronger.

Fallon watched as Julian ignited his Aventi and swung
at Marc's charging form.   The white blade whistled
through the air and inches from Marc's head...it stopped.
The Kjin were at full power. Julian's Aventi was useless.

A look of shock crossed his handsome features, and then he shrugged and used his fist instead, sending Marc Ellis flying against the wall.

He must have realized then the grave danger he was in, but instead of going back out the door, Julian fought the pull of the eddy and used his enhanced strength to sprint around the circle of Kjin to her side.

"Oh, Julian," she cried. "You shouldn't have come."

He reached up to grab the chain and floated directly above her body, their faces inches apart. "Of course, I would come."

"How did you find me?"

"I realized that you would need my help more urgently than a trip to Buffalo. When I got back to town, it was impossible to miss the foul energy coming from this building. Well, for an angel as talented as me, anyway," he teased.

She smiled through her tears. "We both go, then. Back to Emperica together. It will be just like old times. And, we can see Blane again."

He let go of the chain with one hand and shoved his Aventi down her shirt. "No. Just me. You have to continue the fight. I'll tell Blane you said hello. I love you, Fallon." He kissed her lips. "Mmm...I always wanted to do that.

Then, his other hand came free of the chain, and his body flew toward the opening of the gateway. As he passed through the line of Kjin, he reached out and grabbed one around the neck. The demon screamed out as he followed Julian into the pulsating white light.

Upon contact with the purity of an Emperica link, the Kjin was shredded to pieces, and with an agonized scream, both he and Julian disappeared from sight.

Everything went silent and still, and Fallon's body fell to the concrete floor.

It was hard to believe that Julian was gone. Gone for good from this earth he loved so much. He gave up his life to disrupt the deadly Ha'Basin, and he took his infectious smile, her tears, and her will with him. He left her with nothing. She was an empty husk. She could not even bring herself to care when Marc Ellis started cursing and shouting, his mouth full of blood.

"Couldn't you idiots stop him? He was one Knight and we were at full power! Now, we need another blackcoat before we can start again!" He started pacing when no one offered a response. "Tyras is not going to be pleased." He looked directly at a middle aged Kjin who looked like he would fit right in coaching his child's soccer team. "Who can we get on such short notice, George?" Instead of answering Marc's question, the Kjin removed a cell phone from his pocket and began punching in numbers.

Marc strode to her while the Soccer Dad Kjin tried to solicit another blackcoat. "Any more surprises before we begin again, Knight?"

She just stared at him blankly. She had nothing left.

He lifted her chin with one hand and gazed into her vacant eyes as his other hand slowly slipped inside her shirt. She never so much as flinched when he pulled out the Aventi that Julian had given up his human life for her to have. "I will take this. You will have little use for it where you're going."

෨

Fallon's mouth twitched up in a wide smile. She was standing among the high grasses of a picturesque river valley. Butterflies fluttered freely around the trees and colorful wild flowers dotted the landscape as far as the eye could see.

Although the vista was stunning, Fallon's smile was not for the beauty of the valley. It was for the man who suddenly appeared at the top of the rise.

Kade.

Her brave Kade.

A dimpled-smile painted his handsome face as his eyes found hers.

With a yelp, she ran to him, and he threw his head back and laughed before hurrying down into the valley to meet her. Fallon picked up her speed, anxious to be in his arms again.

She began to cry as she ran. She missed him so much. She could not remember why they had been apart, only that she needed to feel him again.

Fallon ran and ran, anxious to reach him before he disappeared from her life again. The muscles in her legs burned, but she ignored the pain, wanting only to close the distance between them. Glancing down for a moment to avoid a rock in her path, she looked back up, and he was gone.

She stopped and spun around frantically, searching for him. Where did he go? *Kade! Kade!*

The realization suddenly came to her that he was gone for good this time, and she knew why. It was her punishment for failing so badly. She invited Kade into her life and it cost her hers. Not only her life, but the lives of untold others who would now suffer at the hands of Kjin she should have been destroying. She selfishly elevated her own desires above the needs of others.

Still, she was desperate to see him again. Father Tomas assured her that love was a gift she should embrace. If only she could see him one last time.

Kade! I need you!

"Shh. I am here."

Fallon's eyes popped open and she gasped loudly. But, the furious beating of her heart slowed when she saw that she was still in the warehouse. Her aching arms still stretched over her head in chains. It was just a dream. There was no valley. No butterflies. No Kade.

She slumped a tear-stained cheek against her shoulder. No, not a dream. A nightmare.

Another anguished gasp tore from her throat and when it did, a familiar smell wafted to her nose. Spicy soap. She swung her head up.

"I'm here, baby," he whispered from behind her at her throat.

"Kade?" she whispered, turning on the chains to get a look at him.

There he was. Dimpled smile and all. And, now he was going to die just like Julian.

"Kade, you have to go!   There are too many blackcoats. Please, Kade, I could not stand to watch you die."

Not after Julian. And, Father Tomas. And, Anthony.

"Nobody is going to die," he told her confidently. "I'm getting you out of here."   Standing from his crouch behind her, he studied the locks around her wrist.

"How? You don't have a key."

"I happen to know a thing or two about locks. Now, quiet."   From his pocket, he pulled a slender pin and inserted it into the lock. After a few seconds of working it around the mechanism, Fallon heard a click and one handcuff came free.   It only took him another few seconds to free the other hand.

She wanted to rub her wrists, but they were too tender to the touch. She found relief instead by rubbing away the prickling pain shooting up her arms. Nothing ever felt so good in her life. It meant she was alive.

"How did you get in here?" she asked him.

He pointed up to the ceiling in the far corner behind her. A duct vent was hanging open. When he helped her to her feet, she threw her arms around his neck. "But, how did you know I was here?"

Kade scratched his head. "I don't know exactly. I felt the presence of a large, black cloud hanging over this building, and I knew something evil was happening here. It wasn't a real cloud, just a feeling I had." He shook his head. "It was weird."

Fallon released her arms and looked at him. *My little Intuit.* Although he did not have the inner sight to see paranormal activity, he could sense it. "You are a very special man, Kade Royce."

He kissed her lips. "Keep that thought until we get out of here. Come on."

She stumbled as she tried to take her first steps, but Kade grabbed her before she could fall.

"I need a chair," he said, scanning the room.

"No, we don't," she said. She staggered over to the open vent and stood directly beneath it. "I'll go up first and pull you up." When she noticed the look on his face, she said, "Just deal with it, Royce."

He smiled. "Actually, having a superhuman girlfriend is kind of growing on me."

The door banged open.

"There!" shouted the Soccer Dad Kjin, and three blackcoats piled into the room and sprinted toward them.

Fallon bent into a crouch and jumped straight into the air and through the open vent. Landing smoothly in the tight space, she leaned back down through the hole and stretched her arm toward Kade. "Hurry! Grab my arm, and I'll pull you up."

Kade jumped, but not high enough to reach her.

"Kade! Hurry!"

He jumped again and this time she managed to catch his wrist. She breathed a sigh of relief and with a forceful yank, hauled his body upward.

But, Kade screamed out before she could pull him all of the way through the opening, and he was ripped out of her grip and slammed to the floor. Then, his body disappeared underneath the flailing arms of the Kjin.

CHAPTER 20

Sacrifice

Without hesitation, Fallon dropped back down through the vent to the floor. With a snarl, she reached down, picked up two of the Kjin by their shirt collars, and threw them off Kade.

Kade scrambled to his feet and the other two Kjin stepped back, wary now of Fallon.

Kade was breathing heavy as he put his back against hers. "What are we going to do?" he asked, as the four Kjin regrouped and formed up in front of them.

"I am going to fight and you are going to get out of here. As long as they haven't established a Ha'Basin, I can take these four. At least long enough for you to escape."

"Are you forgetting something?" he asked her.

"What?"

"My conditions? Well, condition, I should say. If you'll remember, I rescinded one of them. You know the white—"

"Kade! Your life is at stake here!"

"So is yours, and I'm not leaving you."

"What in great Tyras is going on?" It was Marc Ellis, and his face was a thundercloud as he entered the room followed by the remaining four blackcoats. "Ah, I see my nephew has joined us. How very convenient for me. You see, I was going to visit right after I was finished here. Aren't you going to say hello to your uncle, Kade?"

Standing back-to-back, Fallon could not see Kade's face, but the bitterness in his words was unmistakable. "You are no uncle of mine, demon!"

Marc Ellis laughed. "This *demon* has been in your life for as long as you have been alive, young man. You seemed to like me well enough for all these years."

"My eyes are now open, demon."

"Not for long," Marc growled at him. "You have no chance at survival, nephew. The Knight is strong, but without her Aventi, she cannot kill the nine of us together."

"At least *you* will die," Fallon hissed at him and felt immensely pleased when Marc's features paled slightly. But, he quickly recovered.

"You are going to need more than the two of you to kill me, my dear."

"How about the three of us?"

Every eye in the room whipped toward the voice coming from the open door behind them.

Nikki!

Wearing all white, the angel slammed her Aventi against the Kur on her arm and the room filled with a brilliant white light. It was the most beautiful sight Fallon had ever seen, but she did not have time to enjoy it as the room erupted into battle.

Together, Fallon and Kade fought the Kjin that rushed to close with them, but it was the formidable angel in white that drew all eyes. Every thrust of her Aventi left a trail of black ash as every Kjin in her path died. Her movements were graceful, but lethal, as she moved like a dancer through the room in fulfillment of her oath to the majestic realm of Emperica. She was a warrior Knight in all her wrath.

"This is the day of the Creator!" she screamed out, thrusting her Aventi into the air. "Your message has been received, Tyras, but you are wrong! Earth is not yours! You dare to declare war on Emperica? I tell you now! We accept! Ephesians 4:27 'And give no opportunity to the devil!' And, so we shall not!"

Ducking a swing by Marc Ellis, Fallon had to smile at her friend. If Darius was watching now, he would be very proud.

With renewed faith and a forceful kick to the chest, Fallon sent the Kjin leader flying across the room to land hard on his back. A quick glance at Kade, showed that he was holding his own with the Soccer Dad Kjin. The Anthony Kjin was already lying at his feet unconscious.

Nikki glided over to join him and stabbed her Aventi through the once sixteen-year-old altar boy and then again to finish off the evil shade. She also destroyed the Soccer Dad with two lightening quick jabs of her blade

It was over.

All except Marc Ellis.

Fallon stalked toward him as he scrambled backward on the palms of his hands to escape her.

"Nikki! Give me your Aventi!" Fallon turned her head briefly to catch the sword out of the air and then fixed her eyes back on the Kjin. "Your days of terror are over."

"Mine perhaps, but there will be plenty others vying to take my place."

"I'll kill them, too."

"The Kjin are growing stronger. Soon, they will be indestructible. You have won the battle, Knight, but the war has just begun."

"You heard my friend. If it is war you seek, we accept." Fallon raised the sword over her head.

"Fallon! Don't!"

Kade skidded to her side. His face was ashen and all of the resentment of earlier was now gone as he looked down at the uncle he once loved very much.

"I have to do it, Kade," she said softly.

"Is there any other way? Any way to get my real uncle back?" The sorrow in his voice broke her heart.

"No, not here on earth. But, he will be released to Emperica with the death of his body."

Kade ran a hand through his hair, conflicted still.

She put a hand on his arm. "Marc told me that he was going to take your body after this was over, Kade. If I let him live, he will come after you. He will seek to possess you."

After a brief hesitation, he whispered, "Do what you have to do," and walked away.

"I'll do it," Nikki said and pulled the Aventi from Fallon's hand. "I don't want you to be the one who kills the person who he has always known as his uncle."

Fallon gave her a grateful smile.

There was no faltering in the redheaded angel as she put to death the Kjin who had taken so many innocent lives. "Tell Tyras hello," she murmured as the body disintegrated.

When Fallon turned around, Kade had his back to them as he apparently tried to process all that he had been witness to.

It's too much for him, Fallon thought once again. *He does not belong in my world.*

The realization weighed on her heavily and she sank to the ground and pulled her knees up tight against her chest. "Kade, I would like to talk to Nikki in private if you don't mind. Can you wait outside for a few minutes?"

He turned with a questioning look. He was so achingly handsome, and it tugged at Fallon's heart to see the grief on his face. Grief she put there.

But, he nodded and walked out without a word.

Nikki came and sat cross-legged next to her.

Fallon smiled at her friend. "How did you get here?"

"Julian called me yesterday and told me what was going on. After that, it was easy. I just followed the boyfriend."

Fallon blushed. "You were pretty impressive tonight, Nikki. I would not be sitting here talking to you if not for your actions. Thank you."

"The annihilation of this many Kjin in one spot? I wouldn't have missed it for the world. Where's Julian?"

Swallowing back the lump in her throat, she said, "He's gone, Nikki. I am so sorry. He risked his life to save me and got caught up in the Ha'Basin."

Nikki laughed. "Why are you so upset? He's back in Emperica!"

"But, he's going to be a Patie!" she cried. "Can you imagine Julian as a Patie?"

Nikki waved a hand. "I'm sure that Darius will come up with something more for our friend. And, he will be happy to be reunited with Blane." She reached over and took Fallon's hands. "Look. We are warriors, Fallon. We know what the risks are, but we fight for what is right. We fight for those who cannot defend themselves. And, in that fight, we will die. But, the best part of all is that at the end of the road is the glorious Emperica."

Fallon hung her head. "I know."

Nikki narrowed her eyes at her. "Okay, I get it now. There will be no Kade in Emperica."

"Am I that obvious?"

"You love him." It was not a question.

"Yes, I do."

Nikki blew out her breath. "That definitely complicates things, but if you keep your work and love separate, I don't see what the problem is."

Fallon snorted. "He's got this *condition*," she murmured under her breath."

"What?"

She shook her head. "Never mind. It's just not that easy with Kade, Nikki. He knows everything and has this idea that he is going to fight by my side."

"That's ridiculous," Nikki told her, but not unkindly. "As admirable as that is, he is a mortal. We are on the cusp of a very perilous conflict. Our world is too dangerous for a human. Especially, for one you love."

Every word Nikki spoke felt like a spike driving into her heart. Fallon already had the same thoughts, but hearing them confirmed by her friend made them real. She could no longer escape the truth. The only way to keep Kade safe was to walk out of his life. She would have to sacrifice her happiness for him to live. And, it was a sacrifice she would make willingly because she would not gamble with his life any longer.

Tears dripped from her eyes. "Give me your Aventi, Nikki, and call Kade back into the room."

CHAPTER 21

Alone Again

Nikki opened the door for Kade, and he immediately rushed to her side and took her in his arms. "Are you okay?"

She nodded into his shoulder and closed her eyes, inhaling his intoxicating soap scent for the last time. If she had not already hardened her heart with resolve, she would have lost her nerve from the smell of him alone.

He pulled away with a smile. "Here. I found this for you." It was her Aventi.

Oh, Kade, so innocently handing me the tool of your destruction.

She took it and got to her feet, and he stood as well.

"Come on. Let's get out of here," he said. "I have a surprise for you."

She shook her head. "No."

"No? Why? What do you have to do?"

She could not meet his eyes. "Something I should have done a long time ago." Her voice was barely above a whisper.

Kade was having none of it. He lifted her chin. "Whatever it is, I will help. We are together now, Fallon, remember?"

"That's the problem."

"What is?"

"Your condition." She turned from him. "I can't allow you to be a part of my world, Kade. Your life is far too precious to me."

He watched in confusion as she switched the Aventi to her right hand and held it away from her body. "What are you doing?"

She turned back and took a step toward him.

He threw his hands up to ward her off. "Fallon! Stop! What are you thinking?"

She took another step and a sob escaped her throat.

"Fallon, listen to me! I take back the condition, okay? That means I won't be in any danger. Now, put that thing away! Now!"

She continued to move toward him as he backed away from her.

"Fallon, please," he begged. "The condition is gone! I'll take you any way I can get you. If that means allowing you to do what you have to do without interference from me, I'll take it." His eyes were full of hurt. "Please, Fallon. Don't take my memory of you away from me."

With a tortured cry, she touched the Aventi to her Kur and the room lit up with its unique white light.

A tear slipped down Kade's face now, too, but his laugh was bitter. "If you truly loved me, you could never do this."

She took another step.

"Fallon!"

His back hit the wall and he slid to the ground.

She took two more steps and stood over him. "I do love you, Kade, and that is why I have to do this. Goodbye, my love."

"No!"

That was the last word Kade uttered before she waved the Aventi in front of his eyes. When she pulled the weapon away, Kade blinked a few times and then looked at her blankly.

She crumbled to the floor with a moan.

Nikki was at her side immediately. "You did what had to be done, Fallon. It's going to be all right."

She pushed away from Nikki and staggered to her feet. "I have to get out of here. Can you make sure he gets home?" She did not even look his way. It would have killed her on the spot.

Nikki nodded. "I'll come to see you right after."

Fallon fled from the room and the warehouse. She inhaled deeply the first fresh air she had to breathe in two days.

Somehow, through her fog of grief, she made her way back to Oak Street and entered the house.

As soon as she stepped into the foyer, she heard the soft strains of music playing. She did not have a CD player or an iPod, so she knew this was Kade's doing. Then, she remembered the surprise he mentioned. She listened. *Tonight I'm Loving You* drifted down the stairs. *This is our song. He remembered our song.*

She shook her head at the cruel irony. He would remember no more.

He did not stop there. Red rose petals were strewn across the floor and then straightened out to create a path up the stairs. Slowly, she followed the fragrant trial to her bedroom and stopped. In the middle of the room, Kade had spelled out *Will You Marry Me?* with more roses.

In a pain-filled haze, she walked through the flowers over to the CD player and yanked the cord out of the outlet.

The room fell silent.

With a primal scream of agony, she climbed into the four-poster bed and cried until the mental and physical exhaustion of the last two days swept her away.

Sometime later, she felt Nikki slide into bed beside her. It was comforting to feel her angelic presence so close. Several times, Fallon awoke in the middle of the night, and Nikki was there to soothe her back to sleep with soft strokes of her hair.

By morning, Fallon knew that she could not continue like this. She had to keep moving and decided to return to Buffalo right away to see Father Michael for her next assignment. It was all she could do. All she had left.

"Feeling better?" Nikki asked when she entered the room with two cups of coffee.

"As good as I am going to get."

"I wish I could tell you I understand what you're going through, but I don't. I've never been in love before."

Fallon was surprised. Nikki always seemed so worldly to her. She thought for sure, the auburn-haired beauty had had many boyfriends in her past. "Never?"

"No, and if it hurts this much, I think I'll pass."

For Nikki's sake, Fallon decided not to tell her that it also came with incomparable euphoria, a sense of wellbeing and belonging, and a shelter from the storm. It was better that she not know and never have to endure what Fallon was going through.

Nikki had a plane to catch back to Cleveland, but promised to visit soon. Fallon numbly embraced her friend and thanked her for her being there. She wished they lived closer together, but Nikki had her duty in Ohio and Fallon had hers here.

After her friend left, it did not take Fallon long to erase the signs of her presence in the old Victorian. It never did. She cleaned up the petals and the rest of the house and finished packing her belongings. With a last look around, she hefted her pack over her shoulder and walked out into the early morning. It was a short walk to the bus station, and there she would be able to purchase a ticket back to Buffalo.

She turned to make sure the front door was closed tightly and when she faced forward again, her breath caught in her throat.

Kade was walking out of his house with one of his roommates.

Both of the men, oblivious to her suffering, acknowledged her with a short nod of greeting and continued to walk down the street.

Her wounded heart, already fragile, shattered into a thousand pieces that ricocheted inside her chest like slicing glass. The urge to turn and run back into the house and hide from the pain in the solitude of her bed was persuasive, but she fought it. She had to accept her life for what it was. She was alone again. Father Tomas, Julian, Kade. They were all gone. She was alone and the sooner she accepted her fate, the better off she would be.

Heading in the opposite direction of the only man she would ever love, she walked out of his life for good.

CHAPTER 22

The Notes

An insistent tap on Fallon's door woke her from sleep. She had been doing that quite a bit lately—sleeping. It was the only time the anguish went away.

It had been two months since she left Alden, but she was still finding it difficult to care very much about anything. Mechanically, she did all that was required of her, but she derived no real pleasure from her life. It almost felt as if she was living underwater where the smallest of movements required tremendous effort.

She often wondered what Darius was thinking. Did he regret now that he had chosen her for his elite team of warriors? Did he wish it was her instead of Julian who fell victim to the Ha'Basin?

The knock on her door sounded louder.

Who could be knocking on her door? She had no friends except Nikki, and Fallon knew she was on assignment somewhere in New England. Her rent was paid, so it could not be her landlord.

She decided to ignore whoever it was and instead threw the covers back over her head and snuggled deeper into her soft haven.

A third bang on her door finally drove her out of her bed. *Someone is going to get a piece of my mind*, she thought as she stomped toward her door.

Rising up on her tiptoes, she peeked through the peephole. No one was standing there. Unlocking the door, she yanked it open and stepped out to look both ways up and down the hallway.

No one.

What is going on here? If this is a prank, some kid is going to pay for it.

With a frustrated sigh, she turned to go back into her apartment and that's when she saw them. The notes. Two sticky notes were hanging on the outside of her door. She tore them down and went back into her apartment. As she headed back to her bedroom, she began to read.

I wanted to give u time to realize what I already know. We belong together. You were right, I am special. It didn't work.

In case you forgot, this note is from the guy who is going to bring you back down to earth.

P.S. Look outside.

A cry ripped from her throat and her knees buckled. She grabbed the side of the wall to support herself as the tears she thought long gone ran unchecked down her cheeks.

"Kade!"

Pushing away from the wall, she walked unsteadily down the hall. "Kade!"

She started to run, tripped over a pillow on the floor, and then stumbled against the window. Afraid that her mind was playing a trick on her, she hesitated. Could it be true? Unable to stand it any longer, she tore away the curtain and frantically shoved the window open.

She looked down to the street.

There he was.

Kade. Her Kade. Leaning against his Jeep Wrangler with his faded jeans and dimpled smile.

He held a placard in his hand that said, "Will You Marry Me?" in red.

Their eyes met and in that moment, she knew she would never be alone again.

More tears sprang from her eyes, but they were tears of joy now. "Yes." It was barely audible, but he heard her. He dropped the card and rushed to the stairs to her apartment while she fell to her knees and waited.

She waited for her life, her love, and her everything to come into her heart once again.

EPILOGUE

Blane

Blane stood looking down at the scene taking place on earth with a smile. Fallon and her new husband were exiting the church where they had just married. Family and friends, including Nikki, stood on the walkway outside of the church waiting to congratulate the couple and pepper them with rice.

He turned when he felt another presence behind him.

"That man is going to make a fine Knight one day," Darius commented, pointing to the wedding party. With a swipe of his hand, the image disappeared.

"Where's Julian?" Blane inquired.

"Tending to the gardens with the other Paties."

Blane laughed. "How long are you going to let the poor man suffer?"

Very uncharacteristically, Darius also smiled. "Not long. I plan to have him at my side to train the new Knights."

"Good. He will be very happy to hear that."

"I expect so. He is a warrior in his heart and soul, and I would not want to waste his talents." The Elder suddenly grew somber. "Tyras is growing stronger, Blane. We need more Knights—stronger Knights—in this battle or all will be lost."

"How did he manage to cross his barrier into earth, Elder?"

"We have our theories, but are not yet entirely sure. One thing you *can* be sure of is that the Creator will stop at nothing to ensure that Tyras never sets a scaled toe on earth ever again."

Blane nodded through his frustration. It was taking him far longer to achieve Knight status than his other friends. All he wanted to do was put his training to use and destroy the Kjin that were wrecking so much havoc on his beloved planet.

"That is one of the reasons I have kept you back for so long."

Blane turned to him with raised eyebrows. "I don't understand, Elder."

"The extra years of training you have had was necessary. You have developed the skills you will need to guide your fellow Knights. The path of the Knight can no longer be a solitary one. The Kjin have organized and so must we in order to defeat them. We need strong leaders who have the physical and spiritual strength to stand in the face of evil." The Elder placed a large hand on Blane's shoulder. "You are that leader."

"But...but, I'm not even a Knight yet."

"On your knees," Darius ordered gently.

Blane immediately dropped to the ground and lowered his head.

"Angel of Emperica, I hereby call you to action as it is your time for battle. Take up your Aventi and let your destiny begin. By all that is good, in the name of the Creator, I name you a Knight of Emperica."

Darius touched his head, and Blane gasped as a fortifying and powerful energy surged through his body.

"Make the preparations, Knight. You are headed back to earth."

CONTINUE THE ADVENTURE:

ANGELS OF THE KNIGHTS - BLANE (BOOK TWO)

ABOUT THE AUTHOR

Valerie Zambito lives in upstate New York with her husband and three children. A great love of world building, character creation and all things magic, have led to the creation of the first book in her Angels of the Knights paranormal fantasy series. Her website is **www.valeriezambito.com**.

Other Books Published by Valerie Zambito:

Angels of the Knights - Fallon (Book One)
Angels of the Knights - Blane (Book Two)
Book One: Island Shifters - An Oath of the Blood
Book Two: Island Shifters - An Oath of the Mage
Book Three: Island Shifters - An Oath of the Children
Classroom Heroes